I
Like the sweet apple which reddens upon the topmost bough,
Atop on the topmost twig, – which the pluckers forgot, somehow, –
Forget it not, nay; but got it not, for none could get it till now.

II
Like the wild hyacinth flower which on the hills is found,
Which the passing feet of the shepherds for ever tear and wound,
Until the purple blossom is trodden in the ground.

Sappho - "One Girl"
(Translated by Dante Gabriel Rossetti)

CONTENTS

INTRODUCTION

Dr Sam Hirst

The link between the literary supernatural and the queer goes back at least as far as the eighteenth century (and likely a lot further). One of my favourite forms of the supposedly true ghost tales collected in seventeenth and eighteenth century compendiums is the that of the three-day return pact. The tale of Major Sydenham and Captain Dyke is a perfect example: two friends, united in life, who swore a pact that whoever died first would return. Ostensibly, what is at stake is a question of life-after-death, cynicism vs. faith, proof of the transcendent.

However, it's hard not to read between the lines, especially when a heart-broken Captain Dyke waits for desperate hours in an appointed garden meeting spot for the man he always calls 'my major'. The Major's eventual return is no less suggestive: message delivered, he seems unable to leave, lingering in his living friend's bedroom. Now, I could well be accused of forcing a queer reading on the tale, but it seems to me that ghost tales like this have always had the potential to reveals loves stronger than death itself, however those loves are

6

understood. Ghost tales have long been a way of telling hidden stories— of all kinds.

The eighteenth century also saw the rise of the Gothic, and the Gothic has queer roots. It dates back to Horace Walpole's *The Castle of Otranto* (1764). Walpole, like a number of prominent early Gothic writers, such as William Beckford and Matthew Gregory Lewis, was, or is speculated to have been, queer. Queer is the best term we have here. The categories that exist today did not exist in same form in the eighteenth century. They are more modern impositions on the infinite variety of queer lives that are lived, have always been lived and were certainly being lived in the eighteenth century. The Gothic is haunted by the queer lives that it ruthlessly tried to supress.

The queer roots in the biographies of their authors emerged in the Gothic novels of the period and their exploration of queer desires and identities. Matthew Lewis' *The Monk* (1796), the tale of Ambrosio whose pride and lust lead him from the pinnacle of holiness direct to the devil himself, is a perfect example of the early Gothic's exploration of 'transgressive' sexuality cloaked in the seemingly heteronormative endings that the period demanded.

Ambrosio's journey from the heights of chastity and sanctity begins with an unwitting attraction to a young novice, Rosario. Heteronormativity appears to rear its head when the young novice is revealed to be the lady Mathilda, but such certainties are once again removed when Mathilda is revealed to be a demon: gender unknown. The novel plays around the edges of gender fluidity and homoerotic attraction, perhaps most notably in its loving and lengthy description of a very naked and very hot Satan.

However, a veil of heterosexuality is pulled over the conclusion with its triumphant celebration of heterosexual marriage for our heroes and the downfall of its alarmingly queer protagonist.

Ambrosio is but one of many queer-coded Gothic villains. The Gothic and horror have always had a propensity for queer-coding their villains or overtly depicting them as queer, from the pleasure-loving Dorian Gray to the secretive Jekyll. All the worst phobic stereotypes have their outings: asexually coded villains whose 'inability to love' or disinterest in sex is a sign of their incipient 'inhumanity': bisexually or pansexually coded villains whose interest in all genders makes them fickle, corrupt and insatiable; trans villains whose identity is pathologized into homicidal desire. Some texts are unequivocally queerphobic but many hold in tension two possibilities: the rejection of the queer versus the covert exploration of the transgressive (and today a joyous reclamation of the villains made in our image). The vampire is a case-study in point.

The vampire has always had a tendency to queerness, from John Stagg's bisexual lead in 'The Vampyre' (1810), to the homoerotic tension in John Polidori's 'The Vampyre' (1819), to the clear lesbian coding in 'Christabel' (1816) by Samuel Taylor Coleridge or Sheridan Le Fanu's *Carmilla* (1872). In each case, the queerly coded vampire plays the villain but the tension remains.

In the case of *Carmilla,* the erotic tension between Carmilla and her victim/lover Laura is depicted as a sort of corruption. However, there is a clear fascination with this form of 'infectious immorality', the sapphic desires which saturate the text, and which escape it. Laura's father and his accomplices might kill Carmilla but she never truly leaves Laura, who remains haunted by her memory.

Carmilla's multiple resurrections, both in productions which exploit the queerness of Carmilla for the heterosexual male gaze (*The Vampire Lovers* – 1970) and those which centre queer creators and queer story telling (*Carmilla: The Web Series* – 2014-6), prove that sapphic desire is not eradicated with a stake to the heart, however easily its avatars may be vanquished with one.

The vampire, permanently on the transgressive border between life and death, villain and victim, monstrous and human, was a natural figure on which to write the conflicted conceptions of the queer which echo through works like *Carmilla* and *Dracula* (1897). It is also the figure which has been most comprehensively reclaimed and reimagined by queer writers—a tangle of ideas of desire, transgression, exile, alienation, community, tragedy and joy. From the non-sexual biromantic vampires of Anne Rice, to the trans vampires of K. M. Sparza, the lesbian vampires of Jewelle Gomez, to the poly bisexual vampires of ST Gibson, vampires and all the baggage and possibilities they bring with them have been requeered. Turned from villains and caricatures into complex human subjects and often darned sexy ones.

Queer writers and creators have always been a part of the genres of the supernatural (Gothic, horror, fantasy), right to the root of it, but today we are at the centre of a reclamation. The crowd with their pitchforks crying 'deviant' is the monster that haunts the edges of many stories. The outsider is reclaimed as a member of our community. The ghosts are no longer silent. Queer creativity, though, is not bound to reclamation. The stories in this book explore the potential of the supernatural tale to reclaim characters but also to place queer people at the centre of the genre itself—as villains, heroes, anti-heroes, side-characters. The stories provide us with celebrations of queer love for our times.

The supernatural tale allows for the exploration of fear as well as desire, to rewrite the world in the colours of our nightmares and our dreams, to imagine love and hope and uncertainty and tragedy and terror and adventure and the unutterably creepy … and all with queer characters, lives and loves, in all their richness, front and centre.

DR SAM HIRST is a researcher in the Gothic, historical theology, and queer writing. They work at Liverpool University and run the Romancing the Gothic *project—free online classes in Gothic and Horror open to all. Check out the project at www.romancingthegothic.com.*

TOGETHER FOREVER

Evelyn Freeling

As the pastor drones on, I tilt my pounding head towards the sky, a slab of pure cobalt stretching over the cemetery as far as the eye can see. I grimace as Jen's mom rubs my back, slicking my black dress against my sweating skin. It's not her fault. At least, that's what I tell myself as I force a wan smile, slip my sweater off, and fan my hand at my face, cooling myself against the sweltering sun.

Jen would absolutely hate this.

She was born and raised in the Yukon, the second coldest territory of Canada. Dreamt of Hollywood and California sunshine all her life, but when she finally got here, she spent every day complaining about the heat and longing for home. That was Jen for you. Incessantly discontent, as if being dissatisfied breathed life into her.

My only consolation at this moment is that she'll spend eternity rotting away under the hot sun she so despised.

I brace myself as the pastor prompts me to make my eulogy. Normally, I think I would do this in a church, but Jen was atheist and her parents don't want to *disrespect the Lord*. Their words. It should be her parents making the eulogy, but they insisted I do it. *She loved you so much, Ellie.* Again, their words.

Hands trembling, I clear my throat. All of her people are here. Her family flew all the way from Canada. Her agent, publicist, everyone who's ever worked with her—every director, co-star, producer—stands before me. Even the college friends she burned bridges with years ago have slinked out of the woodwork. I would've preferred to bury her alone, if only so I could spit on her coffin, but here we are. All together. They watch me expectantly, waiting for me to play the grieving girlfriend, but I'm not Jen's girlfriend anymore, I haven't been for an hour since before she died technically, and the tears won't come.

I bury my face in my hands.

Shit.

Behind the black curtains of my closed eyes, all I can imagine is coming home two nights ago, opening my apartment door, and standing on the threshold. Jen sat on the couch a few feet from where I stood. Her head lolled over the back of the sofa, the top of her skull blown wide open, her scalp turned to pulp and clinging to her long brown hair. Blood and brain matter splattered across the brand new taupe carpet runner I had spent half a grand on one month prior, and the white wall beyond.

I didn't cry then either. Instead, I screamed.

"You bitch. You stupid, petty bitch!"

She always had to have the last word.

I can do this. I have to do this. Taking a deep breath, I squint at the chicken scratch I scribbled on a scrap of paper last night, while I was shitfaced. Regretting both the years of my life and the bottle of Elijah Craig that I wasted on her, I read the cocktail of half-truths and blatant lies I concocted.

"We're here today to remember Jen. Anyone who had the privilege of knowing her would say she was a special person who lit up every room she walked in. She was funny. Passionate about her art. Relentlessly empathetic to others."

It's a load of crap. I know it. They know it. Her acting was hardly art, and she did it for the money and attention. She could be funny, I guess, but usually in a way that was borderline-cruel. I almost choke on the last part, because Jen was about the most self-absorbed person to ever exist. Literally, there could be famine in some faraway country and Jen would find a way to make it about her. Yet, everyone nods along, dabbing away at the tears sliding down their cheeks.

I can feel Jen grinning from beyond the grave, listening to me aggrandize her, and that makes me want to puke.

"Anyone who knew her would also know that Jen was unwell. She suffered from mental illness her entire life. Depression is a cancer. It ate away at her for years until she couldn't stand it any longer."

Jen didn't suffer from mental illness, she reveled in it. She drank herself to oblivion almost nightly. I can't count the number of times I had to carry her back to our car, or drive around Los Angeles looking for her, praying I didn't find her passed out in a ditch somewhere.

I begged and begged her to get help, but she would laugh and say, "Everyone has depression. If you don't, you're lying or you're not paying attention. This is who I am. I have to live with it and so do you."

She didn't suffer. She didn't struggle. Sometimes I doubted she was truly depressed. Sometimes I thought she liked the demand her perpetual downward spiral put on me. I know how that makes me sound. I know I'm not supposed to think these things, not about someone who's killed themself, but it's the truth. At least, my version of it. Every morning after I saved her from her drunken antics, she would beam and throw her arms around me. *My hero.* That was what she called me. Her hero.

"In her memory, I would like to ask everyone to support your local mental health organization with a donation. Let's make sure this isn't the end of Jen's story. Let's turn this tragedy into something good, even if only a little."

Everyone nods along.

I take a final look at her closed coffin, at the maple grain refracting my pale, dry face, and silently wish her an eternity burning in hell. When I return to the row of mourners, Jen's mom hugs me. I want to slap her, to tell her she raised a monster and she shares the blame in all of this, but I don't. It's not her fault. Not really.

Just like it isn't my fault.

Jen only wants me to feel it is.

After I told her we were over, that she needed to pack her things and be out of my apartment by the time I arrived back, just before I slammed the door in her face, she swore I would live to regret breaking up with her. She had threatened it before, every time I tried to end things with her. I admit, I no longer took her seriously, but am I to blame?

No.

I'm not, Jen. Taking your life was your choice. It's not my job to live with it. I don't feel guilty. The only misery you've inflicted is that I have to spend the rest of my life pretending we were still together in the end, so nobody else will blame me. Maybe none of us will say it aloud, but I'll say it to you, if you're out there somewhere:

Good fucking riddance.

After her funeral, I return to my apartment for the first time since I found the body, and the paramedics carted her off to the morgue. Silence weighs down the air, the door creaking open with a high-pitched whine. Her blood spray and chunks of brain block the entrance, as though she's laughing at me from beyond the grave. I'm supposed to wait for the cleaners to come, but I can't. This is the toll I must pay to enter my own home. I drop to my knees and roll the runner up, march down the hall towards the window on the opposite end, and throw it open. Light and warmth stream through. Already, I feel better. I toss the carpet out and only think to glance for pedestrians afterwards. Filling a pot with soapy water, I spend the next hour scrubbing Jen off of my walls and out of the raw wood floorboards, suffocating on the fetid sweetness of her innards, putrefying for days.

It wasn't always bad. Relationships never are.

We had our good times, but in hindsight the warning signs were always there. On our second date, before her career blew up, we went to a movie. She was embarrassingly obnoxious, loudly remarking about the special effects, shouting at the characters. I hid behind my hand as the people around us glared our way. It was only halfway through that I realized she was wasted. That should have been the end of it for me. I don't remember why it wasn't, why I wrote it off.

There's a splash of blood the size of a quarter that's soaked into the wood for good. My lease on this apartment isn't up for another six months. Maybe my landlord will show me sympathy. Maybe if I go into all the gory detail of discovering my girlfriend dead—

"Ex-girlfriend," I correct myself aloud.

I give up on the stain and rinse my hands in the sink, washing the last pieces of Jen down the drain. Now, I can put her behind me. Once and for all.

I crawl into bed. Sleep is the best remedy for most things. I should feel better than I do. I'm free now, aren't I? It doesn't feel that way. It's as though she's still here, lying next to me, whispering in my ear, "If you don't blame yourself, why are you so afraid everyone else will?"

I wake up to a finger of moonlight moving across my closed eyelids. Not moving, flickering, as if something or someone is pacing next to my bed. My eyes peel open. I strain my ears against the rush of blood in my head. Floorboards creak. Or perhaps it's the walls, expanding and contracting. The flickering light, merely a palm tree outside, swaying in and out of the moonbeam. That's it, I think, closing my eyes and willing myself back to sleep.

The bed rustles and sinks, as though someone just lay down next to me. My skin tingles along the bare crook of my neck, across my collarbone, like a phantom hand tenderly grazing me. I leap out of bed, onto my feet and stand there panting, skin still tingling.

I know that touch. It was the same way Jen would wake me up to make love. She'd trace her fingers from my collarbone down to my belly button in … My stomach tingles now, a slow concentric circle drawing smaller and smaller towards my navel.

Screaming, I bolt into the bathroom. The lights buzz on. I press my back into the wall and watch the brass knob of the door, half-expecting it to jiggle and rattle. Mercifully, it doesn't. I sigh and collapse to the white and black tiled floor, dizzy with fear.

Of course she isn't here, haunting me. If she could, I'm sure she would, but I don't believe in crap like that. Do I? No. Of course not. It's all in my head. This is exactly what she hoped for. I imagine her now, crouching in front of me, her green eyes sparking with glee as she sneers, "If you don't feel guilty, why are you afraid I'm still here?"

I balance myself back onto my feet and splash cold water against my face. As I pat it dry, my face buried in a hand towel, eyes closed, something cool breezes against my shoulder. A breath, blown through narrowed lips. I shiver and can't stop as I lower the towel and raise my eyes to the square mirror in front of me. Only the shut door, the light switch, and a bathrobe hanging on the wall.

No Jen.

No shit, Ellie, I tell myself. Jen is dead. Gone. Forever.

The exposed bulbs around the mirror quiver. I brace for the dark, but they glow back on. It's all in my head. I can tell myself it isn't my fault all I want, but true as that may be, it doesn't prevent me from feeling guilty on some level. Strange. I haven't once wondered what more I could've done for her. I'm fairly certain I did everything I could. Yet, here I am, jumping at every sound, picturing her next to me, snickering, whispering, "We'll be together forever. You'll never get rid of me now."

I can even smell her amber perfume.

Clearly, my guilty subconscious is playing tricks on me. A call to my therapist will sort that out. For tonight, I need to sleep. I lumber back into my bedroom, but hesitate to climb into bed. Now, whenever I look at it, I remember Jen telling me countless times how much she adored it, how safe she felt sleeping in it. She owned a mansion in the Palisades, but stayed with me most nights, always complaining how alone that palace made her feel. A few years have passed since she first slept over, the shape of her body is practically embedded into the mattress now.

There's no way I'm going to fall asleep tonight. Not here.

I spring for the nearest motel. Technically, it's the second nearest. The motel that's a mile closer is tainted. Jen and I stayed there for a week after a pipe in the apartment above mine broke and flooded my ceiling, long before she ever bought her house. This place is a run-down little shithole, tainted with many things, I'm sure, but at least not with her.

A television with basic cable, a wardrobe, and one bedside table with a lamp whose bulb seems ready to give up the ghost any second now. I leave it on, hoping it will last long enough for me to fall asleep.

Before I can rest my eyes, my phone trills.

I glance at the clock and groan. One in the morning. Who in the hell would call at this hour? A number I don't recognize. Of course.

"Hello?"

"I figured you wouldn't be able to sleep at night," a woman says.

My body empties. I swear I can feel my soul lifting out of me, drifting to the ceiling. Whoever this is, she sounds just like Jen. There can't be reception in hell, though. Can there?

"Excuse me?"

"I can't sleep either."

"Who is this?"

"Judy."

Jen's mom.

"Oh," I say, already wanting to hang up. "Hi. How are you?"

"Are you seriously asking that question?"

I almost have to laugh. It is an asinine question to ask someone who's grieving.

"Look," she sighs. "There is a point to this call. I thought about what you said today and you're right. I want to do something, to make some good of this. Well, I wanted to. I made a donation to this organization, Colors? Have you heard of it? They help provide mental health services to people like Jen. Like you."

"Queers?" I snort.

"Er … yeah, exactly. Anyway, my donation was quite sizable, but they said I could do even more for them by doing a spot of publicity. Raise awareness. I can't bear to do it. You know how I am with that kind of stuff."

I really don't. Jen barely spoke to her parents. I met them once before she died, over an awkward hour-long dinner at a Chinese place.

"Well, you were so wonderful today, and you were so much closer to Jen than I was in her final years … I really think it ought—"

"I'm sorry. I know what you're going to ask, but I can't. I just can't."

She falls quiet. For a moment, I think she hung up, but she sniffles, breaking our shared silence. She's crying. "I should've tried harder. To stay close to her. I keep thinking … if I had, maybe—"

"Judy, it wasn't your fault."

"Then whose was it? Who could've prevented this?"

Me.

"Nobody," I say.

"Nobody? I just can't accept that, don't you understand? I have to believe she could've been helped. I have to believe that we can help the Jens who are growing up now."

She thinks Jen killed herself because she was troubled, because she was bullied in high school. It's laughable. She was gorgeous growing up, never had an awkward stage to speak of, prom queen. Troubled, sure, but she killed herself out of spite. Revenge. I don't have the heart to tell Judy though, and more than anything, I want to sleep.

"What do they want me to do?"

"An interview. Tomorrow. At her place."

"Fine."

"You're an angel. Be there by noon?"

I blow out air, feeling absolutely defeated. "Sure."

Dial tone.

She refused to let me go in life, but somehow Jen's chokehold on me in death is stronger, even more unrelenting. I shut my eyes and fight myself to sleep.

Screeeech.

A scratching at the curtained window sends a chill dancing down my spine. I won't let her frighten me for the rest of my life. I throw the blankets off and march to it. Hand wrapped around the ugly floral printed fabric, I hesitate.

Screeeech.

Do I want to know? Perhaps it's better to suffer the noises of the night, wait them out until morning. There's no unlearning what you already know.

Screeeech.

Bracing for the worst, I fling them open. Standing before me is a pale woman, bedraggled, circles dark as merlot under her eyes.

I sigh, shaking my head at myself. With the dying light behind me, the darkened window is a mirror. I cup my hands against the cold glass and strain my eyes through the night. A half-empty parking lot, half a dozen sleeping cars, a palm tree swaying in the breeze.

I imagined the sound, just like I imagined Jen climbing into bed, initiating foreplay with me from the afterlife.

Stepping away from the window, I freeze. My reflection and the one of the room behind me swims back into view. Looming over my shoulder, her brown hair bobbing next to my blonde, is Jen. Her lips part into a sneer. She unfurls her arms, laces them around my waist. Every hair on my body stands on end as my skin warms under her touch. I whirl around, but find myself alone.

"Jen?" I call, voice catching in my throat.

Silence.

I'm losing my shit. That's it. Add this to the list for my next therapy session. Still, something inside me is unconvinced. I can feel her near, relishing in my torment. My heart won't slow. I hurry into the bathroom and draw a hot shower, let the water scald me back to reality, burn Jen from my memory.

That's all this is.

Memory.

I haven't been alone, truly alone, in so long, she's like a phantom limb now that she's gone. I only think I can feel her presence because she welded herself into my life, into me. Toxic as our relationship was, it doesn't change the fact that Jen was a part of me for years. Now that she's gone, because she is, I need to give myself a little grace.

That's all, I decide as I dry myself off.

I turn to wipe the steam from the mirror, but shudder to a stop, my blood curdling in my veins. Scrawled on the mirror:

E + J forever.

With a heart for a period.

The air turns to lead. I can't breathe. I claw at my throat, gasping futilely. She's never going to leave me. She's so demented, so possessive, she has managed to defy the laws of physics, of biology, of heaven and hell.

Stumbling over myself, I race around the room, tugging my clothes on, forgetting my shoes and wet hair. I burst outside, scramble through the parking lot and put as much distance between myself and the hotel as I can.

I don't sleep. I drive. Up and down the Pacific Coast Highway, from Dana Point to Malibu and back, until the sun peeks over the canyon and casts its soft morning light onto the waves breaking below. Avoid glancing in the rear view mirror the entire way, dread like a boulder in my chest.

I sit in a coffee shop. Watch the clock on the wall count the seconds. Every so often, the second hand stops in place, as if time is glitching. I can smell her, feel her enveloping me, even with all these people around. Strangers brush against me as they pass. I jolt. They apologize, shooting me perturbed glances.

A woman with a pink pixie cut and thick false lashes walks in, sits at a table across from mine. She reads a tabloid. On the cover is a headshot of Jen, a headline in bold white letters—JEN CAMPBELL, DEAD AT THIRTY. The woman uses a napkin to dab at the tears cutting rivers through her makeup.

"Strangers are mourning me better than you did," Jen hisses in my ear.

Or maybe she doesn't. Maybe I'm hearing things. People do that when they snap, don't they? Realizing the time, I race to Jen's place in the Palisades. Judy will never forgive me if I don't show. I shouldn't care. I don't know why I do.

Wincing as I walk through the oversized front door, I take the mansion in. Last week, we had a horrible fight. A blow out. The kind of fight that would've necessitated neighbors phoning the cops if they were within earshot, but the properties in this neighborhood sprawl for a half-acre each at minimum.

It's just as I remember it. The foyer enters into a wide open space that connects the living room with its huge white brick fireplace, a dining room with a sculptural looking chandelier and the kitchen complete with an island and two ovens. Blown-up portraits of Jen line the walls, mostly from her favorite magazine spreads. Everywhere I move, her eyes follow me, glinting with accusation. Floor-to-ceiling windows peer into the backyard. One of them still has a massive hole, commemorating the escalation of our worst fight, when Jen heaved a chair at my head and narrowly missed, thanks to my reflexes.

I can't believe we have to do this here, but the camera crew has already arrived. A woman with glasses hurries me to Jen's office, where hair and makeup have set station. I ask them to keep it basic. The makeup guy smiles sadly as he explains he's using waterproof everything. They're going to be disappointed if they're banking on tears from me.

He rambles on as he flutters a soft-bristled brush over my face, about what a fan he was of Jen's work, how sorry he is for my loss.

There's no polite way to tell someone to shut up, but under his incessant chatter a noise pricks my ears. I shoot my hand up and he falls silent.

A woman screaming.

Distantly. Muffled. And … it sounds as though it's coming from below us.

"Do you hear that?" I ask.

He listens, frowning. "Hear what?"

"That woman. That scream."

I stand and wander out of the office, ignoring his pleas to be reasonable, that I'm not finished, that I still have rollers in my hair. As I wind into the living room, her voice grows closer, clearer. Though, there are no words to make sense of. Only a never-ending cry of agony. There must be a basement or something. A wine cellar.

That would be very Jen.

I wander in a daze, opening every door I can find, searching for stairs that lead down, but surface nothing. It makes no sense. This can't be my imagination, though. I can hear her, screaming and howling as though she's being tortured, as clear as I can hear my own voice.

"I'm so sorry, girl. I get how hard this is, I do," the makeup artist says as he drags me to a chair in front of the fireplace and tugs the rollers from my hair. "You're on in three minutes. Please, just hold still so I can finish or it's my ass, okay?"

I nod, still lost in my daze. Her cries are loudest here, by the fireplace. I turn over my shoulder, ignoring his annoyed sighs as I do. It's Jen. I know it's her. She's there, somewhere. I wished her an eternity burning in hell yesterday and now I'm listening to the soundtrack of my wish-come-true. A black and white portrait of Jen glares down at me from above the mantel. I shrink in the chair.

Oh God, what have I done?

Before there's time to answer, a news anchor sits before me. Blinding lights blink on. A fluffy microphone hangs above my head. The news anchor boasts a head of perfectly manicured black hair and a matching suit with a crimson tie. He narrows his eyes at me as someone announces that we're rolling.

Oh God, what am I doing?

"Ellie Simpson," he says.

"Uh-huh."

"You were Jennifer Campbell's girlfriend for how long?"

For the first time, I notice Judy, leaning against a wall behind him, her arms crossed, eyes shimmering. She holds a tissue at the ready.

"Let's see … " I try to think. I know this. It's easy. "Over three years. Almost four."

"How did you meet?"

"A friend introduced us at a gallery opening."

He waits, wanting more, but that's all I have to offer.

"And what was she like?"

"You know … Normal, I guess."

"Down to earth?"

I snort. "No. She was normal, like … she could be charming and fun, but she had her issues. Just like everyone else. Money and fame didn't change that."

"What sort of issues did she have?"

It would be easier to list the issues she didn't have, but before I can say so, Jen's screams erupt from the fireplace once more. I shudder and twist in my seat. There must be a way down. She needs help.

"Ellie?"

"Excuse me?"

"What sort of issues did she have?"

"You know. Body image issues. Eating disorder. Drugs, sometimes. Drinking all the time. Depression. Usually her depression was caused by drinking. She could be wonderful, but she was imperfect, just like anyone. But she was also functioning. Which made it harder to help her."

Her screams rise an octave. I leap to my feet and storm to the fireplace, fumbling my hands over the bricks, looking for a lever, a concealed button, anything.

"Ellie?" the anchor calls me.

"What?"

"Please sit. We're not finished."

"Don't you hear her?"

"We'll get to that in a moment."

"What did you say?"

"I said, we'll get to that in a moment."

I turn, slowly. My knees wobble, unable to hold me up much longer. What's happening to me? I fall in the chair, limbs going numb. This is wrong. This is all wrong. The anchor's lips widen into a

Cheshire grin, all horizontal, no tilt upwards. His dark eyes gleam, reflecting the red of his tie.

"How many times did she warn you?"

"Warn me what?"

"That she would kill herself if you broke up with her."

"I-I-what—"

I glance to Judy for help. She wipes the tears from her face, but doesn't come to my aid like I hope.

"How many times, Ellie?"

"I don't know. I lost count."

"And what did you do that last time, when you finally abandoned her?"

"What do you mean?"

"Did you call anyone? Did you ask anyone to be with her, to keep an eye on her?"

"Well, I thought she'd be fine."

"So, you didn't."

"It wasn't my fault."

"You aren't sure about that."

"I am."

"Then why are we here, Ellie?"

I shake my head. Her screams crescendo. The bricks in the fireplace rumble. Plaster rains from the ceiling above. There's something wrong with me. This isn't happening. It can't be. Outside, the sun dips below the horizon, casting a red, hellish hue across the sky that falls inside, carving out the hollows of the anchor's face.

"This is what you wanted—"

"No."

"You wanted her gone. Dead—"

"No!"

"Out of the picture—"

I slap my hands against my ears and squeeze my eyes shut. This isn't happening. I've snapped. I'm trapped in a hospital right now, probably wearing a straitjacket, lost in my own mind. That's rational. This—

"The day you buried her, you told her to burn in hell."

"I didn't mean it. I was angry. I was—"

"Open your eyes, Ellie. Now."

I shake my head. "No."

"Guards."

A set of burly hands pry mine from my ears. A grating din shakes the ground below me, like metal grinding. Another set of hands pry my eyelids open. We aren't in Jen's living room anymore, but a dungeon of some kind. Stone walls lined with shackles. Jen's screams are louder and shriller than before, echoing all around us. The man sitting across from me has shed his suit for a judge's dress, a white wig atop his head. Sitting next to him, Judy. Tears drip from her chin, fat as raindrops in a storm. Her eyes are cold and gray as she regards me.

"How do you find the defendant?" he asks.

"Guilty," Judy replies, her eyes burning holes into me.

"We hereby sentence you. For life."

"No!"

My scream blends with Jen's. Sweat slides down my face as flames erupt around me. They crackle and jump, licking my skin. Something touches my hand, cool against this unbearable heat. I turn and find Jen, her hand wrapped around mine, her jaw unhinged in a mirror of my own, but she isn't screaming. Over the sizzle of my own flesh melting, I can hear her cry, "Together forever, Ellie. You and me. Together forever."

EVELYN FREELING is a lifelong writer and a member of the Horror Writers Association. Her short fiction has been previously published with Ghost Orchid Press and Dark Dispatch. She was born and raised in the Pacific Northwest, but currently haunts Dubai. When she isn't writing or reading, she's probably being tormented by her terribly wonderful two year old. You can find her on Twitter @Evelyn_Freeling.

BREATHE INTO THIS

Kristin Osani

Shiran reaches through the car's shattered windshield and holds the balloon to the dying man's lips. "Breathe into this, please."

He looks up at her, rheumy eyes cracked with red. When he inhales, pieces of his crushed lungs rattle in his chest. For a moment, Shiran fears he might not manage enough to inflate the balloon, and she will be forced to reap his spirit without securing his final breath for her collection. Her flesh crawls with centipedes at the thought, but she *cannot* be late to this delivery.

The man blows out, and the centipedes settle as the balloon puffs up into a fist-sized purple egg. Shiran pinches off the latex, wipes a thin pearl strand of reddened spittle from her thumb, and places a palm on the man's damp brow. It takes as much force as tearing open a sweet wrapper to peel his spirit from his body.

Adorned in the white shinishozoku and triangular diadem of death, the man's spirit comes to crouch beside Shiran on the hood of the car. He stares at his corpse as it lists to the side in the driver's seat.

31

"My son was wrong." His voice is gravelly with bravado. "Wasn't the smokes that got me after all."

She stops herself from telling the man of the cancer metastasizing in his bronchial tubes. It is not against the rules, but she has learned it's wiser to speak to spirits as little as possible, and only ever with crisp, professional politeness. Fewer openings for them to try to flee, or play on her sympathies to strike a bargain.

Somewhere beyond the field of rippling rice stalks, an ambulance bleats in futile desperation. Shiran ties the purple balloon off with a deft twist and strings a slender ribbon around the knot. The balloon bobs up in the air just over her shoulder.

"Come with me, please." She unclips a miniature oar from her obi; it grows and elongates in her palm until it's large enough to bear Shiran and the spirit both. "I must deliver you to the Yellow Springs."

The spirit scratches under the white circlet perched atop his wispy combover before mounting the oar behind Shiran. His arms tighten around her waist when the oar lifts into the sky.

They sail over the countryside, over fruit-laden orchards and jagged mountains and towns tangled in telephone wires. The spirit says nothing except for the occasional observation, muttered to himself in an incredulous mantra, that he is really, truly, dead.

Shiran clutches the string of the balloon between her palm and the smooth wood of the oar handle. She ignores the spirit and ponders where in her home the balloon will be most comfortable. It may do well in the cluster of foxtails. Or perhaps on the short bridge that arches over the moon pond. Or—

"You said the Yellow Springs." The spirit interrupts her musings. "Do you mean Paradise?"

"I mean the Yellow Springs. There you will drink of their cleansing waters and be taken on."

"On to Paradise?"

"On."

"Could just say you don't know," the spirit grumbles.

They descend between shrugging peaks and wind through a narrow gully diluted with fog. Fingers of mist curl up from the earth and tug at their vestments, Shiran's many-layered black and the spirit's thin white. Prismatic butterflies flit between crimson clusters of spider lilies. The spirit shivers and presses himself against Shiran's bony frame, but if he's hoping for warmth there, he will find none.

The rock garden gets the most sun. Shiran reasons that will be a fitting place for her newest companion.

One more gentle curve through the mossy bluffs, and they arrive. They dismount the oar. The soft loam gives a little under Shiran's sandaled feet as she leads the spirit up the short path to the Yellow Springs.

A series of steaming pools the pale saffron of sunrise nestle between the sprawling roots of the fig tree towering above them. The air stings of sulfur.

Beneath the sulfur, Shiran scents the rotting earth stench of demons, the time-obsessed imps, ready to drag reapers to the mercies of their domain for the infraction of a single missed deadline. They are forbidden from entering the Springs, but have taken to crowding the boundary whenever a reaper is delivering.

Shiran supposes all attendants of the Yellow Springs find ways to bend the rules without quite breaking them, to cope with the wearisome nature of this work.

She motions the spirit to a wooden ladle perched on a flat stretch of roots. He wrings sun-spotted hands for a few moments before taking the ladle up.

"I lived a good life." His chattering teeth mince the words. "Not perfect, but good."

Whether or not these claims are true isn't Shiran's job to judge. She gives the spirit a small nod of acknowledgement all the same, hoping to encourage him to be quick about it so she can go home. The purple egg jitters anxiously beside her.

Nodding does the trick. The spirit kneels, dips the ladle into the springs, and brings it to his mouth.

"I lived a good life," he says again, and drinks.

Her job done, the delivery made, Shiran turns away.

The rotting earth stench vanishes. Its abrupt absence is an angry wail. Shiran's thin lips part in a smirk, imagining the demons gnashing their teeth over being denied the pleasure of punishment yet again.

A solitary peak in the reapers' domain is where Shiran rests between deliveries and curates her collection. The curved eaves of her house cut ambivalent smiles into the pink sky. Its slatted windows seem to squint in satisfaction as she ascends the stairs into a courtyard flooded with balloons.

The purple egg drifts shyly back with every step Shiran takes. The balloons ripple at her passage, bend towards the newcomer, create waves of curious whispers when their skins rub against one another. No two are ever alike. Their uniqueness, Shiran thinks, must be why she risks precious moments collecting them before reaping the spirits, stoking the demons' ire with each near-delinquency.

A bed of white gravel sprawls behind the house. Basalt boulders jut up above the small pebbles like onyx glaciers. Here, too, crowd balloons; the sunlight filtering through them splashes kaleidoscopic patterns on the enclosing plaster walls. Shiran ties the purple egg to a carved lantern in the southern corner, fingers lingering lovingly on the string. The balloon whirls happily in the breeze, and she smiles.

Inside her living quarters, she slips out of her sandals, brews some bitter tea, and indulges in a sweet red bean bun. The soft murmuring of her balloons is her only company. How she wishes she could understand them. Speak with them.

There comes a gentle tug on her awareness. Another delivery. Shiran lets the last bite of the bun melt away on her tongue, sweet and slow, as she rises to her work.

The oar takes her over highways clogged with cars whose headlights bleed yellow and red onto the asphalt. Shiran alights on one of hundreds of identical high-rise balconies. She shifts through the sliding doors and steps inside the one-room apartment with a limp stirring of blackout curtain.

On the crumpled sheets of the narrow bed within lies the young human whose spirit she has come for.

The sweet-yeast scent of cheap beer sways against Shiran's nose. Clutched in the human's left hand is a half-crushed can. More cluster on the low table in front of the television, in the tiny kitchenette sink, on the floor beside the overflowing recycling bin.

It is not Shiran's job to judge. Still, she cannot help the pang of pity for this human and their apartment of empty cans.

Shiran kneels beside them. Their long hair spiderwebs out in a black halo beneath their head. Their suit is wrinkled, the first three buttons of their plain white blouse undone. The curve of their stomach twitches in slowing undulations as their internal organs drown in alcohol.

Their gummed eyelashes flutter when Shiran brings the balloon to their slender lips. "Breathe into this, please."

Dark brown eyes cross as they focus on the balloon, before teetering up to meet Shiran's sober gaze.

The human laughs.

Shiran blinks.

This is not the reaction she was expecting.

Still laughing, the human hoists themselves up onto their arms. Their head lolls heavily to one shoulder. They reach out a hand. The beer can tumbles from their grasp as they draw cold fingers down Shiran's face, tweak one of her conical ears, trace the curve of the velvety horns protruding from her temples. Shiran is too bewildered to stop them.

"Shit." Their words slur around the edges. "At least my death is beautiful."

Shiran reclaims some composure. "There is no such thing as a beautiful death."

The human's clumsy fingers comb through her bright crimson hair. "Then what are you?"

"Your guide."

"My guide." They repeat the word like they are tasting it for the first time.

"Yes." Impatience gnawing at her, she lifts the balloon to their lips once more. "Breathe into this. Please."

A petulant frown contorts their features. "Why? What's it for?"

Her fingers clench around the slippery material. Words clump and tangle in her throat. She has never needed to explain. Not to anyone else, not even to herself. "To hold your final mortal breath."

One of the human's thick eyebrows carves into their forehead. "And you need that to guide me? To the afterlife?"

"It is unrelated."

Their lips twist. "You mean it's just for shits and giggles."

"It is not—" Shiran stops. Tries again. "It is more than—" Rolls her tongue between her sharp teeth. "I collect—"

"It's fine. We all need a hobby. I get it."

Shiran nearly melts with relief, but when she lifts the balloon a third time, the human jerks away.

"Wait. What'll you trade me for it?"

"*Trade*?" Shiran rises, spreads wide her arms and absorbs into the folds of her black reidōi the ambient light of the static on the television screen, the stars and moon and streetlights outside. Darkness thick enough to suffocate on douses the room. It galls, knowing her professionalism slipped enough that she must resort to this amateur scare tactic. "Humans do not *barter* with attendants of the Yellow Springs."

"This one does," comes their defiant retort, no louder than a rabbit quivering. "If you want their last breath for your morbid little balloon collection, anyway."

Shiran reins in her annoyance. Stubborn mortals have tested her before. She always prevails.

Bit by bit, Shiran allows the light to leak from her reidōi whence it came. The television crackles back to life, casting a static glow over the human's brown skin. Their dilated eyes are fixed up at Shiran, shoulders squared, fists gripping the bedsheets by their hips.

She bends low over them, hovering her empty hand centimeters from their forehead. "I could reap your spirit without it."

"You could." A bead of sweat trickles down the human's neck, spills over their clavicle and disappears past the fraying collar of their blouse. The salty tang of their fear singes Shiran's throat. "But I don't think you will."

Her black enameled nails scrape delicately along the human's cheek, catching on the edges of their spirit. The human exhales swiftly, their chest stilling. The muscles above Shiran's lip twitch.

She should make good on her threat. She has dallied far too long already. She can hear the demons cackling in delight, feel fiery claws sinking into her flesh.

But Shiran has never reaped a human's spirit before claiming their final breath.

She hisses. "Tell me what you wish in exchange."

The human gasps in air, claps a hand to their mouth. They cannot believe they have bargained this far. Neither can Shiran.

"Paris." The word takes a while to squeeze out between their fingers. "I've always wanted to go."

Paris is on the other side of the world, though it is not the distance that matters. There is no telling how long the human will wish to stay there. Shiran suspects it will be well past her deadline.

Despair steals through her like poison. She must refuse, and forgo her balloon.

She has only herself to blame. She should not have given the human time to question, time to realize they hold the advantage and call her bluff.

Shiran stills. An idea strikes her.

Time is the issue, but time is malleable—if Shiran is willing to imbibe the human's blood.

Her stomach churns at the thought of taking something so impure into herself, regardless of the power it holds. It will change her. Irrevocably, if she is not careful.

But it need only be a single drop. That is enough to bring the human to Paris yesterday, leave them to their fun, and return to claim their breath. The fold will be small; the demons should not notice. Even if they do, Shiran will have delivered the human's spirit well before the deadline passes.

She lets her hand fall away. Stands upright. "I will take you for one sunset and one sunrise."

Shiran prepares to argue—mortals always want more—but to her surprise, excitement lights the human's face like the moon cresting over a still lake.

"Deal." They scramble up from the mattress, swaying on their feet and stumbling forward when their toe snags on the lip of the floor rug. Shiran catches them without thinking; the human clutches her forearms, and for the span of several of their finite heartbeats, gazes up at her with an unfettered smile dimpling their round cheeks. "Thank you. Thank you, Guide."

"Shiran." The introduction is startled out of her. "That is what I am called."

"Shiran." The sound of her name on someone else's lips—a human's, no less—is a strange thrill. "I'm Naru."

She doesn't tell them she already knows, only watches them scurry about their room like a frantic fawn. She allows herself a low chuckle at the way they stuff themself into their clothes, elbows and hips crashing into corners, and rams supplies they hardly look at into a satchel. They twist their tangle of long black hair up into an unbalanced bun before turning back, breathless, to Shiran. "I'm ready."

But she is not. She reaches out, takes their hand in hers, runs a light finger down their palm. Braces herself. "I require a drop of your blood before we depart."

Naru shivers, tugs their hand away. Again, they surprise by brooking no argument. They take a decorative pin from the breast of their jacket. Before Shiran can stop them—her nails are sharper, would be less painful—Naru jabs the metal prong into the fleshy part of their thumb with a silent wince.

They proffer the welling crimson to Shiran. "This enough?"

Shiran bends over their hand.

Hesitates.

She does not have to do this.

She has to do this.

She presses her lips to the wound.

Naru gives a hissing gasp. Shiran feels herself begin to stutter and shift as their death settles into her like it belongs there. She grinds her shrinking teeth on a groan of pain. The fabric of her being rearranges. The taste of cheap beer washes over her tongue.

"You…" Sobered, Naru draws hesitant fingers across Shiran's softened features, her small round ears, her hornless brow. "You look…"

"Human?" Even her voice is transformed. Lighter, more airy. She adjusts her clothing—not layered reidōi now, but slender trousers and a silk blouse tucked beneath a double-breasted waistcoat. The only thing that hasn't changed is the length of her hair, smoothed back from her face in an intricate plait.

Naru's mouth twitches as they tug on the black ribbon tied in a loose bow beneath her collar. The casual touch makes Shiran's newly human heart throw itself against her breast. "Overdressed."

"Your blood chose this form, not me."

Their brown eyes dart away. "I wasn't complaining."

A lopsided grin—her lips are unaccustomed to these flat, broad teeth—staggers over Shiran's face. "Then come."

Naru's arms settle easily around her waist as she lifts the oar into the air. Shiran draws upon the human power screaming through her veins, and compresses time around them like crumpling paper in a fist.

When she releases, it unfolds all at once into eggshell storefronts clustered shoulder to shoulder, knotted rues, towering steel.

The city stirs lethargic under gauzy grey clouds. Early risers splash through the shallow puddles pitting the pavement, heads bent low beneath umbrellas, thoughts bent on the warmth of their destinations. None of them notice Shiran steering the oar to the slick cobbles of a narrow alley just north of the Seine.

The toes of Naru's worn sneakers scuff the street, tap-tapping an erratic rhythm against the square-cut stones.

"What are you doing?"

"Making sure it's solid." Swallowing, Naru half-slides, half-jumps from the oar. They land with their hands splayed out to either side for balance, their knees slightly bent and wobbling. They giggle. "Paris. Oh gods, I've died and gone to Paris."

Naru isn't dead yet, and won't be until the blood magic wears off, but Shiran does not correct them. Raindrops encrust their hair, slip down the bridge of their nose. Shiran conjures a large umbrella and holds it out for them to take before their clothes soak through completely. "I will find you this time tomorrow."

Their fingers reach past the umbrella and grab Shiran's wrist as the oar lifts, angles towards the next morning. "Wait."

"One sunset and one sunrise, that is what we agreed."

"I know." Naru does not relax their grip. "And you said you'd take me, not dump me in the streets and fuck off."

A willful misinterpretation of their arrangement. Shiran would rather not wait for the slow turn of the earth to bring them back to sunrise, but she fears Naru will refuse her the balloon if she refuses to stay.

She sighs, fastens the oar to her belt, and unfurls the umbrella over their heads. Naru does not let go, only moves their hand up to settle on the crook of Shiran's arm, their shoulder snug against hers.

Together, they walk out of the alley.

The tedium Shiran braces for never comes.

Naru leads them through the arrondissements like a hummingbird flitting between flowers, drinking heady gulps of nectar. Their blood runs rampant inside Shiran, spurring her to keep pace. The moments blur together without distinction between beginning or end, the only constant their mortal companion.

Things Shiran already knows and has already seen become strange and new for living them: bitter sips of espresso, buttery flakes of croissant, rich chocolate and bubbly wine. Stained glass windows, the

43

smoky scent of burning wax, the shuffling of footfalls gradually syncing. The sharp flap of pigeon wings, stalls full of plastic trinkets and landmarks in miniature, laughter that puts cathedral bells to shame.

Blue cracks the clouds in the late afternoon. Naru crouches down to pick up a crushed violet from between the pebbles of the garden path they wander. One of its petals lilts away as they twirl its stem between forefinger and thumb.

"It's beautiful," discovers Shiran. Naru reaches up to tuck it behind her ear. The soft fragrance envelops her like a veil.

"They probably don't have violets where I'm going, huh?"

Shiran puts her hand to her ear, fingers lingering on the warmth Naru leaves behind. She has never given any thought to where spirits go once cleansed by the water of the Yellow Springs. "They might."

Toying with the hem of their jacket, Naru squints into the golden glow on the western horizon. "I suppose I'll find out."

Something inside Shiran begins to unravel.

They climb a great hill. With each step she takes, Shiran plucks a violet from the air and weaves them together, desperate to stop whatever is coming undone within herself. When they crest the rise, Shiran places the flower crown atop Naru's sweaty brow.

It settles crooked, but Naru doesn't straighten it. Their chin lifts, and their fingers find Shiran's and twine around them like ivy.

The unravelling quickens. Shiran does not know if it is comforting that she can sense Naru coming undone, too.

An insistent wind nips at their ankles with cold teeth, but sulks away when neither of them pay it any mind.

The Eiffel Tower is a charcoal smudge atop the shrouded sea of the city. Shiran feels Naru's fingers pulse as their gaze latches onto it. She does not need words to know that is where they wish to go next. To go last.

The moments blur into the snap of the metro doors shutting, the tinny music of the carousel at the tower's foot, the spinning lights illuminating brown eyes blown wide with exhilaration.

The night flees, cruel and quick. Shiran unravels, and unravels, and unravels, no matter what she does to keep the threads of herself pulled taut. Naru fares no better, unspooling with each turn of the merry-go-round.

As the sky blushes violet behind the steel frame, Naru turns to Shiran in all their drunken glory, their death seeping from her veins. "One more day," she whispers. "One more day, and I'll give you *two* balloons."

Shiran was waiting for this. Mortals always want more.

But now, so does she.

Greedily, she takes their hand, and another sobering kiss of their blood.

The moments blur. Naru's fingers wear grooves between hers. Shiran no longer feels the pain of transformation. The unravelling slows, reverses, until they tangle back up into themselves, and into one another.

She brings them to yesterday again, and again, as many times as they ask. Naru promises her so many balloons, they have both lost count by the time the demons find them.

*

In their rented room in the Latin Quarter, just before sunset, Shiran lurches upright, gagging on the stench of rotting earth. She scrambles from the bed and hunts through her scattered clothes for the oar.

"What—?" Naru tugs their oversized t-shirt up off the vanity chair and down over their shoulders. Their nostrils flare. "It's them, isn't it?"

Shiran is too intent on searching for the oar even to nod. She finds it and doesn't bother to detach it from her belt before willing it to its proper size. The fastener snaps in half with a metallic *ting* and ricochets off the ceiling. Naru lets out a cry, not because the debris has struck them, but because through the peeling plaster above them materializes, upside down, a head.

Broad-browed and eyeless, skin bruise-blue, the demon flicks out its tongue to snuff the air. It moves cockroach-quick, shoulders shimmying out of the plaster, followed by skeletal arms and clawed hands that gouge into the ceiling and heave the rest of its body into the room.

"Foolish reaper." It speaks in a crackling hiss, like the pop of dry kindling. "Did you think you and your human could hide from us forever? Bend time enough, it leaves a *crease*."

A half-dozen more of the imps swarm through the walls and the floor. Naru smashes the vanity chair over one that makes a grab for them, crying out when it scratches the back of their hand. Shiran seizes a fistful of moisture from the air and freezes it into sharp crystals, flinging the ice in an arc at the nearest attackers. Sprays of umber ichor coat the carpeted floor. As the struck demons howl in agony, Shiran pulls Naru onto the oar.

Claws shoot out and scrabble for purchase on the blade, shaving off long curls of wood. Naru, still clutching a splintered chair leg, clubs the imp over its eyeless skull. There is a crunch, and the demon crumples.

Free of their would-be boarder, Shiran takes a droplet of blood from the weeping scratch on Naru's hand and steers the oar down the familiar path to Paris yesterday, trying to buy more time to think. A murky skyscraper unfolds before them, wiry rooftop antennas swaying in the passing breeze.

Naru shivers against Shiran like the last leaf clinging to a wintery bough. "I'm ready to go."

Shiran is not. "We will find a way—"

"You should've reaped my spirit and taken me to the Yellow Springs, I don't know how long ago—but I kept putting off blowing up your balloon."

"That is not—"

The oar pitches and bucks. Shiran barely manages to keep her grip on it as it spins them out of the way of a bright blue blossom of flame.

The snap of the roll breaks Naru's hold around her waist. They tumble backwards, but manage to grab onto the end of the oar. There they dangle, screaming. Shiran twists to haul them back up, but another jet of flame sears her across the face.

Skin blistering, she lets out a roar and plucks up the breeze with her free hand. She whips it into a gale and hurls it out in the direction

47

of the flames. A chorus of cackles sounds, and when she squints through prickling, ashy tears, she sees the demons swarming the sky-scraper in front of her.

"Pathetic reaper," says the one crouched atop a corner edge like a gargoyle. A razor-toothed leer is carved into the angles of its face. Globes of fire the same sickly blue as its skin swirl above each of its clawed hands. "If you're going to flee, at least make it more of a chal-lenge for us to follow."

An imp crawling up the skyscraper's windows makes a teasing swipe at Naru's ankles. They flail their legs, crying out as its claws skitter against their skin. With a snarl, Shiran uses her power to uproot an antenna from the roof and send it spiraling through the demon's chest. The metal pins it to the glass like a grotesque beetle, just as two more of the horde leap through the air and tackle Shiran from the oar.

She is dragged out of the human realm and into the demons' reek-ing domain. The imps wring Naru's blood from her body. She screams as the transformation reverts. It *hurts*, because while her body may no longer be mortal, her heart still is.

It spent an eternity pumping Naru's blood. *That* change cannot be, will never be undone.

Shiran hits hard red dirt, her curled horns gouging deep ravines into it as she skids to a stop. The demons are heavy on her back. They tear her reidōi to the waist, affix a seal along her spine to stymy her pow-ers. Still she tries to draw on something, anything to fight the imps off, and she cries out as white-hot pain flares between her shoulders.

"It is the deepest hell that awaits you, reaper." The demons hiss gleefully in her ears, pressing the seal deeper into her flesh. "Who do you think we can make scream louder: you, or the human?"

And as if the words summoned them, Naru is there, swinging the oar like a scythe. The weight of the demons disappears with a crack of wood against bone.

Shiran howls when Naru scrabbles at the long strip of inscribed paper on her spine, tearing the seal off in strips. They wrench off the last scrap and manage to drag Shiran onto the oar as a wave of demons comes crashing towards them.

Delirious with agony and helpless to instinct, Shiran urges the oar towards the one place they cannot be followed. The wave crashes against the boundary moments after they cross with a tempestuous shriek. The sound rages in Shiran's ears long after it ebbs away.

The shrugging peaks, the misted gully, the clusters of spider lilies. Shiran shivers against Naru, feeling like a trespasser. They round the mossy bluffs and step onto the soft loam. The smell of sulfur hails her, and beneath that, rotten earth.

No power can keep either of them safe outside the Yellow Springs now.

In the fig tree's shadow, Naru combs their fingers through the tangles of Shiran's crimson hair, brushes dirt from the front of her lopsided obi.

She presses her lips to Naru's hands, touches her brow to theirs. For several of their precious heartbeats they embrace. They taste of salt, of cheap beer.

"I promised you a balloon."

"It doesn't matter—"

"A promise is a promise is a promise." Their words slur. Their lids grow heavy.

With trembling fingers, Shiran searches her reidōi. It takes her a few moments to locate the balloon. She has forgotten, after all this time, where she stored it.

When she pulls it from its pocket, dried violet petals scatter out around it.

An idea strikes her.

She doesn't know if reapers are taken on to the same place as humans, or if they *can* be taken on at all—but she does know she doesn't want to be trapped here, with a balloon her only company.

She puts the balloon to her lips first. When she blows out, it inflates into a jet black sphere. Careful to keep it pinched shut, she holds it out to Naru. They inhale. Purse their lips around the mouth of the balloon. Exhale. Red marbles the black.

Shiran ties the knot, strings the ribbon, winds it around the root by the ladle. The balloon sways for a moment, then stills.

Naru's legs buckle beneath them. They curl up by one of the roots. Close their eyes as their death catches up to them at last. Shiran bends over them, caresses their forehead with a light touch that betrays the heaviness weighing her every movement. When it is done, she falls to her knees. Naru's white-clad spirit helps her stand.

"We lived a good life," they say, and though it is not Shiran's job to judge, she cannot help but agree.

Shiran dips the ladle into the waters of the Yellow Springs.

Naru's fingers settle into their usual grooves.

Together, they drink.

KRISTIN OSANI (she/her) is a queer fantasy writer who lives in Kyoto, where she works as a freelance Japanese-to-English video game translator when she's not wordsmithing, working on nerdy cross-stitching, or cuddling her two cats (three if you include her husband). Her fiction has previously appeared in FlashPoint SF. *You can find her on Twitter @kristinosani, Instagram @kristin.osani, or her website: kristinosani.com.*

BECOMING

R. Wren

If only he would feed me less, then I could starve in earnest; if only I could starve in earnest, maybe then I could feed myself.

I kept trying to tell him that, my poor, sweet, starving Tommy. Every time he dipped his hand into that black, bottomless pool which never froze over, surfacing with a chunk of bread between his changing fingers, I told him.

"You need it more," I said, as he came to shiver with me under the shelter of the upturned boat. I tutted and touched his chest. Even through the mittens and his heavy woollen fleece, he could not hide his jutting ribs. "Oh, look at you. You look worse than Nod."

He shook his head. "It ain't for me," he answered. "Lookit."

He tore a strip with his fingertips and placed it between his lips, gentle as communion. The food turned to ash and fell away. He took advantage of my momentary confusion to force the bread into my hands. Even gaunt-faced as he was, sunken-cheeked, half-covered in patchy beard and with his eyes retreating back into his skull, my Tommy always managed to look pleased with himself.

"Don't waste it like that," I said.

"But it ain't wasting. I can get more, look."

Tommy moved to go back into the wind. I pulled him back by his shirt-tails.

"Stay. And put back on your gloves before you're frostbitten. That's an order, Tommy."

Tommy stayed. He squeezed my hand a moment, then pulled back on his heavy mitts. We both ignored how his skin shifted and shimmered against the friction of the wool.

We both knew that the real distinction between seaman and officer had dissolved long ago; if it wasn't gone when the ice closed its jaws around the *Acheron*, it abandoned us when the late Captain caught Bosun's Mate Jeffries with a thigh-bone in his cooking pot, but let him walk away into the mist rather than hang him.

"Eat it, then," he urged me. "Go on."

I did.

The bread was wet, almost oily between my aching teeth. Most unnervingly, it was warm. Nobody but Nod ate warm food anymore, as there wasn't enough wood left to burn.

The last time I had a real fire, it was just to thaw the ink bottles. Abandonment, all souls to march west and seek civilization. We left that note under a crudely pushed-together cairn, with no real hope that any soul would ever read it.

"I meant what I said," I urged. "No wasting food. With luck, the caribou will return with the thaw, but we can't take anything for granted."

"It's not wasting, sir," Tommy said, with the tone of an argument he was long tired of. "The hole in the ice will …"

"We can't take it for granted," I repeated. "Whatever it is, it's not natural. It's not civilized."

Tommy gave me a look.

The wind outside our make-shift shelter carried a mock cheer to us. That could only mean that our brief Artic day was starting. I finished the oily meal and went to crawl out into the air. Tommy caught me by the wrist and kissed my cheek; I turned away from him sharply.

"Not here, I told you," I said sternly. "Not in camp."

"There's no naval code here," Tommy said. He fell back onto the black, frozen ground, his baggy clothes swallowing him. I could see his exposed collarbone, the skin turning copper and scaly. He was breathing hard; the mere exertion of stopping me had taken the strength from him. "We're a long way from England."

"You know the rules," I said, but I wavered. His poor delicate skin. I only wanted to reach out and soothe it. "Not in camp. Nowhere the men might see us."

"Yeoman Riley has thrown away his crucifix to worship the pool," Tommy panted. "Nod's grown healthier the more of us die, and the Beattie brothers have gone plain mad. Are those the men whose opinions we're waiting on?"

I didn't answer.

I kneeled and crawled out into the cutting air, to watch the sun illuminate our tattered camp.

Under the rising sun, the wasteland of ice and snow around us became a creeping shade of red. There were no trees to silhouette, no damned trees for miles. There were only jagged black rocks to cast shadows from. The rocks, our scattered stacks of despoiled crates, our midden-heap topped with several human hands, and the few tents which had not yet collapsed. To the west, I could still mark the graves we had dug in a more hopeful time. Back then, breaking the frozen earth had seemed worth it; since then, we'd stolen their markers for firewood.

Only Nod saluted my arrival. He sat cross-legged outside the mortuary tent, whistling and whittling a bone. The others were where they always were; staring into the pool like so many narcissuses.

"Up, men!" I croaked, striding across the crunching ice. I stiffened into the naval posture, one of the many behaviours of circumstance that I wore like an ill-fitting coat. "Who's on watch? Who's on hunting duty? Mister Riley, I ordered you yesterday to move that pile of rifles under shelter. Mister William Beatie witnessed a bear only yesterday evening. If the beast comes this way, will you be glad to find them frozen?"

"With respect, sir, piss off," William Beatie answered. He was on his knees against the unnatural pond, mittens on the ice, peering into the depths. Golden pocket watches dangled from his breast in huge numbers, giving the impression that they were multiplying there. Only a year ago, we would have caned a man for speaking that way. "I'm not afraid of any bear. There's not enough flesh on me, sir, to make me worth his while."

"Not afraid, Mister Beatie?" I barked back. I picked up a rifle by its icy steel barrel and threw it into his arms. "Then go see if you can't take him down. A good bear, even a scrawny one, will put some meat on your bones for sure. Off, all of you! If you keep dipping your noses in that pond, you're sure to be frostbitten!"

"But the water is warm, sir," said Yeoman Riley earnestly, his eyes aglow with religious fervour. "You'd know that if you tried it, sir. What do you see in it, sir? The Beattie brothers can see only gold, sir. Mister Nod won't tell me, and I know your Mister Tommy sees food. I see home, and look at what I found in it!"

He raised a porcelain teacup, something too delicate to have ever survived the death-march from the *Acheron*. I noted that all the fingernails had disappeared from his right hand. The fingertips, like his lank and straw-like hair, were turning transparent.

"It's my Mother's, sir. I drank tea from this cup on the day I left home, sir."

"Give me that, Riley."

The jittery yeoman handed me the mug. I dropped it to the ice, where it shattered.

"Take a rifle, Yeoman, and see if you can't bag us a gull. And Mister Thomas is not *mine* any more than you all are. I'll have no more talk like that."

Yeoman Riley nodded and scurried away. He seemed not at all worried by the destruction of his teacup. I felt confident I would see it again, restored to his changed hands, before long.

I was left alone, now, with the eerie pool of black water. My cheeks were already burning with the cold. I straightened my cap, shielding the tops of my ears under the hair which I had never had occasion to let grow until now. My own beard scratched painfully against my collar; despite all else, I had been most miserable of all when the scarcity of hot water compelled me to stop shaving it.

I felt the tug. Knowing that I shouldn't, I crouched a moment by the pool side.

A face rippled up at me, pale and staring through the water. The phantom's face was not my own, not exactly. It did not blink when I blinked, nor move as I moved. Yet it was a version of me; a gentler, softer portrait, with a feminine slant to the jaw and new life in the eyes. Here was a double who had been spared the Navy barber's shears, a double who had never had to suffer the straight-razor's sting at the throat.

Here was the face I ran away to. I fled it into the service, fled onto an expedition ship, scarpered to the very limits of Civilization ... and here it was, calmly waiting for me beneath the ice.

"So what *does* it show you?" asked a coarse voice from behind me.

I was startled out of my thought. I turned, reassuming the naval demeanour, lowering my voice into the naval growl, gritting my teeth like a man whose boots leave his feet bloody, but who knows he must march.

"Mister Nod," I winced. "Have you no duties to perform?"

"You're the only other one who hasn't been tempted," Nod grinned, revealing the gaps in his teeth. "Just you and me, sir. Fine company, eh? The men without temptation."

The bone-knife he was whittling was still in his hands, blade towards the earth. I did not comment on it; we both knew the bone wasn't animal.

"You've never been tempted by what you see?" I asked him.

Nod laughed. It was a wheezing, hollow, manic sort of a sound.

"Oh no, sir," he said, slapping his paunch. He was the only man to have grown larger since the crew was scattered. "You see, sir, I don't see anything but water. I'm a man of simple tastes, I am. I have everything I want right here."

A shudder passed through me which was not from the cold. Nod slapped my shoulder and wandered away, grinning all the time to himself.

I could not help glancing back into the pool. The image seemed indistinct for a moment, but then the face reasserted itself. I had the momentary desire to cover the water with my coat, but I knew it was pointless, as well as foolish. Our temptations were our own.

I stood watch over camp while our brief mockery of a day came and went. I timed it by my watch; less than four hours, in which the men took sullen pot shots at nothing in particular. My stomach ached monstrously. I pressed my hand against it to silence it. I would not give Tommy reason to return to that ghastly pool.

The land reclaimed the sun. We returned to darkness.

R. Wren

I wriggled back under the upturned boat, kicking my boots against the ground to shed some of the ice. Tommy lay under the blankets, near passed-out with exhaustion. In the fading light, he seemed almost skeletal. I pulled off my cap and crawled in beside him, otherwise fully dressed.

I hesitated for a moment before putting my head against his shoulder.

I felt him stir. "Here?" he murmured, reaching to feel my tangled hair. "In camp?"

I said nothing. Two images hovered before my eyes; the ghostly face, and the vacant, satisfied expression on the face of Mister Nod. If we had any sense, we would have court martialled him long ago. And yet, what was the point now? The talk of caribou was a fairy tale, I knew. This place would be his grave soon, just like the rest of us.

Perhaps just a little later than the rest of us.

"Tommy, would you still welcome me if I were different?" I whispered. My words caught in our hollow shelter, humming under the arching roof. Our upturned boat was like a capsule outside of the world; a private room, or a tomb.

"You mean, if you were a different man?" my Tommy asked. His voice was sleepy and weak.

I shook my head. Tommy lifted himself up on one elbow. I could feel how much he strained to do it.

"If I was simply different," I tried again. My hunger made me desperate and emotional; I felt a stinging in my eyes and rubbed them, knowing that an un-masculine display of hysterics risked freezing my eyelids shut. "If we were born again as souls without bodies, thrown into forms without distinction to class or to sex, would you still know me?"

Tommy relaxed back onto his blankets. He let a heavy sigh, and I worried dearly for him then. I felt his fingertips in my hair; his gentle stroke was answer enough to let me sleep.

At a certain hour, his hands grew still.

When I woke into the stark, suffocating darkness of an Arctic morning, I found that I could not rouse him.

I tugged in vain at his limp, bony shoulders, shaking a body which felt more like a ghastly children's doll, something stuffed full of straw with a skeleton made of twigs. Still, he did not stir. I fumbled for my tinderbox and lit the stub of a candle. Once, it had rested in the Officers lounge aboard the *Acheron*. Now it cast its sickly yellow light over my poor Tommy's sunken face, still as a corpse's.

I put my hand to his wrist. I found a pulse.

Emerging from under our upturned boat without either my hat or gloves, I marched swiftly towards the dark pool. Even at this hour, the surviving men kneeled peering into the water. The dark pool did not reflect their flickering candles. I roared at them, and my voice sounded reedy and hollow to my ears.

"Make way!" I barked. "Has anyone a cup of broth which can be thawed? A soup or a porridge? Quickly, now!"

"Course we don't," drawled William Beattie, standing upright and glittering with gold.

"If we did, we'd soon as eat it!" answered his brother Jamison, likewise adorned.

"The pool will supply you, sir," urged Yeoman Riley. His voice was trembling with holy rapture. "You need only ask it, sir."

I snapped for them to clear the way. This they did, although sullenly and with delinquent slowness. They would go no further than was required to let me approach the pool, and there they stayed, watching with naked curiosity.

I dropped to my knees at the edge of the pool. The pale, womanly face watched me without consideration or judgement, unleashing a burning discomfort to wash through me, bone-deep and stinging. I pushed it aside. I thought of my poor, fading Tommy. I willed the pond to offer me what I needed.

"Your Tommy must be next to go then, eh?"

I turned away from the water and saw Nod just outside the candles' glow, sat cross-legged atop the crate of rifles. The crate was just where I had left them before the sunset; clearly nobody had followed my order. I struggled to conceal my revulsion at the man.

"He most certainly is not." I said.

"I reckon he is," he grinned.

"I will hear no talk of that kind, Mister Nod," I said, gritting my teeth. "Certainly not from you."

The Beatie brothers cooed in delight. Nod only shrugged and turned away to conceal some private smile.

"You only have to take it, sir," Yeoman Riley said, falling to his knees beside me. He took my arm and guided it towards the pool. "Just reach out and take it, sir!"

Their eyes on me were intolerable, and as much to escape that as anything, I allowed my fingertips to breach the surface. I recoiled at the feel of it; not flowing like water, it was rather thick and rolling like fat. It had an all-too-lifelike warmth.

Without even looking, my fingers found something hard and cold. Pulling it up, I produced a chipped porcelain bowl overflowing with broth. The broth was thick and steaming. It filled my nostrils with the smell of beef. The Beattie brothers watched on, murmuring among themselves.

Saying nothing to my men, I turned and hurried the bowl back to the upturned boat where my Tommy lay senseless. The liquid lapped at the rim, spilling here and there to sizzle on the packed, frozen ice. My fingers tingled with some indescribable sensation; they seemed to shimmer as I moved.

It was then that I realized something peculiar; I was holding the very bowl from which I had often eaten my supper as a child.

I found Tommy as I had left him, the candle still burning low. I was breathless and electrified with terror and hunger combined. I tried to force a sip on him; I tried to rouse him with the smell, or spoon the meal between his unmoving lips.

It was no use. He would not be roused.

I tried in vain throughout the inescapable arctic night, long after the broth went cold. I only stopped when I felt his cheek, and my spirit froze to feel that he was going cold, too.

With my changing hand, I set aside the bowl. I put my head against his chest and lay there, alone in our private tomb.

When I finally crawled out to face the others, I found Nod and the Beattie brothers already standing outside our boat. I did not need to tell them that Tommy was gone. Mister Nod was already waiting with his freshly whittled bone-knife. The wind whipped through our raggedy camp, causing them to squint over their scarves and collars, and causing William Beattie to shield their lone candle, whose flame glittered in the gold which hung from his breast.

The sky yawned over us, black as the water below or the merciless rock between.

"He's gone then," Nod said. "Ain't he?"

"We'll dig a grave when the ice thaws," I said weakly. They must have seen the ice clinging to my cheeks. "It's the honourable thing."

"You know we won't make it to the thaw," William Beattie said, his voice muffled through his scarves. "Not with honour such as that."

"There ain't no caribous," growled his brother. He was holding a rifle in his hands—his bare hands. The metal ought to have stuck to and torn his skin, but the coppery scales which had grown to cover his hands seemed immune to the cold. "There ain't no bears, and there ain't no gulls neither. That pond'll give us gold and trinkets, but there's nought to trade it for—and it's changing us. We all know it."

"And eating flesh won't?" I demanded.

Nod shrugged and scratched his jaw with the handle of his bone-knife. "Better the devil you know."

I stood alone against them, the upturned boat and Tommy at my back.

"Take the broth," I pleaded. There fell the last shreds of hierarchy, I thought; no more orders would be given or obeyed. "Take it, and give me time. Let me say goodbye. Give me that."

The Beattie brothers shared a look. Jamison shifted the rifle in his arms. He looked almost embarrassed to be holding it.

"Hell, I'll take it," said William. "I'm not going to turn down any sort of a meal."

I babbled my thanks then, bowing and raising my hands in a manner that would have disgraced any officer. I crawled back under the boat and found the broth. It was dry in here, and almost warm; the candle had burned almost all of its wick.

With shaking hands, I took a fistful of Tommy's blankets and held them into the flame. In just a moment, they began to smoulder.

When the first real flame erupted, I threw myself out the far side and onto the ice. I heard cries of confusion from the other men; only when the first puffs of smoke and licks of flame appeared from under the boat did they realize what was happening.

The Arctic blackness enveloped me and I ran, the wind scattering the heavy crunch of my boots. The camp lay in darkness, and I had no light, no hat or gloves. I trusted my bearings. My Tommy burned behind me. In any civilized world, he would have been buried—but the civilized world was far away, behind a wasteland of ice and a ceaseless night, and the concerns of that world were no longer mine to uphold.

The flaming boat and panicking men were behind me, now; I struck a taut stretch of fabric and felt a tent pole snap under my weight. Already I could feel the wind biting at my ears. I reached out to feel my way, but the hand which had not touched the dark pool had gone numb. I felt with the other, and the world felt new and strange.

"Here, sir!" cried the close and fervent voice of Yeoman Riley. "Turn this way, sir!"

I ran towards his voice, trampling over the camp detritus, the artefacts of order which some future expedition might pick over. I reached out with my changing hand, as though I could feel the eerie water which had marked it.

"Here!"

I stumbled onto my knees, landing beside the strange little man at the edge of the pool. I could hear the other men rampaging somewhere nearby, but I knew the night would conceal us.

The woman's face looked up at me from the pool. My face. Even in the darkness, I could see her.

"You only have to reach out, sir," Yeoman Riley said. His voice was close; I could feel his breath on my skin. "It will provide. You only have to reach."

I looked further. There was another face under the surface, gasping for breath; one sunken and hollow.

I plunged both hands into the water. I met another hand, one which clung to mine like a drowning man. I pulled. His other hand found me.

65

I dug my heels into the ice and hauled with all my strength, but my strength was not as great as it had once been.

A candle-light danced somewhere nearby. My hands were warm and alive. Boot steps marched toward us. I heard somebody testing the bolt of a rifle.

"Don't fight against it," Riley urged. "*Reach.*"

I rolled forward on my knees and plunged into the pool.

The water filled my ears; it filled my lungs. I opened my eyes and saw nothing. I felt his hands in mine. I felt my hands changing. I felt everything change, and then a flickering candle passed over the pond, and the dark night's sky was afire with lights I could never see before.

I emerged onto the ice to shouts and cries. I pulled, and my dear, loyal Tommy stepped out with ease.

He stood taller now, or seemed to, to me. His hollow cheeks and jutting ribs had not changed, but now they seemed beautiful. His skin shimmered and glittered with green and gold; he was like a creature of copper, or the lights in the night above.

I felt my face, and found it soft like the sky.

"What in the name of God?" cried old Nod, tumbling back onto his rear. He scrambled away from us, and I could feel his fear. "Where did they go? What are … ?"

Jamison Beattie took aim with his rifle. The barrel belched fire which shone in his gold. My Tommy flinched, but I calmed him with a hand on his shoulder.

I led him by the hand and we turned, disappearing away over the ice.

There I ran with him, beautiful and strange, trailing copper-coloured hair which scattered in the wind. We skimmed over the mountaintops and feasted on the sky. Somewhere nearby, wicked men starved. They were creatures of Civilization, I told him. They could not follow us now.

R. WREN is an Irish writer of weird tales. They collect and create scrap paper in all its forms. They write because they don't believe in ghosts, but wish that they could. Their twitter can be found at @ro_wren.

THE ONLY THING TO FEAR

Caitlin Marceau

Gwen pulls the flyer off of her locker and frowns. It's the same as all the other ones that have been posted around the school: a duck egg blue background, the darkened silhouette of a teen mid-transformation, and bright, pineapple-yellow words scrawled across the top. 'THE ONLY THING TO FEAR IS SHAME ITSELF!' the paper reads, in a thick marker font. She rolls her eyes at the date written at the bottom of the poster, and waves the paper in her friend's face.

"Are they *really* making us all go to this assembly today?"

"Technically, it's two assemblies—the juniors are having theirs this morning and we get ours this afternoon—but yes."

"Ugh," she grumbles, spinning the dial of the lock clockwise, "it's so boring. It's not like we don't already know about this stuff. Mr. Ryan gives the same speech every single year. We practically know it by heart."

Roisin leans against a nearby locker with a smile, tucking a strand of her curly red hair behind her pierced ear and peering at her friend through her lashes. "I, for one, am excited for today's assembly."

"That's because you get to skip French, which you suck at."

"*Bien sûr, mon amie*," she laughs.

"Think there's a way I can sit it out?" Gwen asks, rummaging through her bag as she looks for her math books.

"Now why would you want to do that?" asks a voice from behind her. The boy wraps his arms around her waist and hugs her from behind, planting a kiss on the back of her shoulder. "Not only do we get to miss the boring lecture on Sappho, but we can sit in the back of the auditorium and spend the entire assembly making out."

"Wow, Mateo, that sounds like so much fun," Roisin says drily, crossing her arms in front of her chest, her smile no longer reaching her eyes.

"Don't worry, you're not invited."

Gwen turns to look at him with a smile, dislodging herself from his grasp. "I have a feeling Ms. Rileigh is going to make us sit with the rest of class."

"A man can dream."

"And that's all he can do," Roisin mutters under her breath.

Mateo glares at her before turning his attention back to Gwen. "Anyway, I've gotta run. I'll see you in English." He leans in and kisses her quick on the lips before she can pull away. "I can't wait for tonight."

He waves to his girlfriend before turning his attention to the gaggle of boys down the hall, and Gwen lets out a breath she didn't realize she was holding.

"You're seeing him tonight?"

"Uh, yeah. We're just gonna hang out and watch movies."

"Mhm."

"Did you want to come over too?"

Roisin's laugh is more like a bark. "I'd rather eat glass. Besides, I don't think I'm invited. He's never liked me." Gwen opens her mouth to disagree, but she hates lying to her friend, so instead she stays quiet. "I thought you were going to break up with him? What was it you said? 'He's definitely not my type,' wasn't it?"

"I don't know. I was thinking about it. What we have right now is fine…"

"But?"

". . .but he keeps pushing for more, and I guess I'm not ready for it."

"You're not ready for more, or you're not ready for more *from him*?"

"I don't want to talk about it."

"Gwen—"

"I don't want to talk about it." Gwen shuts the door with a sigh, hooking the combination lock through the metal loop and snapping the shackle closed.

"Whatever," Roisin says, heading lazily to class. "Come on, we're going to be late for math."

Gwen spins the dial on her lock one more time and follows her friend.

"I just don't get why we keep calling them werewolves when they're not werewolves," the blonde girl says, with an exaggerated sigh. Her friends in the row beside her snicker, as do some of the boys sitting behind her. Gwen rolls her eyes at the question and shifts in her seat. Mateo's hand is hot on her thigh, and she wants nothing more than to swat it away. He looks at her with a smile, so she smiles back and puts her hand on top of his.

"Well, they're not called werewolves," Mr. Ryan—the school's senior health and wellness teacher—answers, trying to keep his annoyance from showing. "They're called loups-garous or rougarous, and wolves have nothing to do with it. Every transformation looks different, even if they do all happen between dusk and dawn. Some people have canine-like features, while others resemble boars, owls, or even cats. Remember, we're trying to end the stigma surrounding loups-garous, especially when two out of every five students your age will experience an outbreak. Perpetuating this werewolf—this *monster*—stereotype only does more harm than good. When we're talking about loups-garous, what's the most dangerous thing?"

"Shame!" the audience yells back, well-rehearsed in this speech. Gwen stays quiet and crosses one leg over the other, hoping the change will dissuade Mateo from keeping his hand on her.

Success!

He takes his hand off her leg and instead leans towards her, wrapping an arm around her shoulders. She's somehow made the situation worse.

"Exactly. It's why establishing healthy relationships with your family and friends is so important during your high school and college years. Because while adult outbreaks are still common—one in six adults will have at least one experience of turning into a loup-garou between the ages of twenty-five and sixty-five, and one in eight will continue to experience outbreaks well into retirement—they impact almost *half* the population during adolescence."

Mr. Ryan takes a seat on the edge of the stage, his white sneakers squeaking against the wood as he arranges himself more comfortably. His green track suit with the school's logo—a knight holding a lance and a shield—blends into the background, painted the same green with the same logo. He carelessly bangs the microphone against the floor, staff and students cringing from the loud noise, before turning his attention back to the audience to answer the same questions he gets every school year.

"Yes, Geoffry?"

"Is it true we have to draw blood *and* recognize the person to cure them from being a rougarou? 'Cause, like, bruh, I don't want to hurt my friend." People around the auditorium laugh, including Mateo. Gwen doesn't get what's so funny.

"No, that's just another misconception, much like the one that becoming a loup-garou happens when you miss Easter for seven years, or fail to observe lent. Undergoing the transformation only happens to students who are dealing with immense shame. A shame that's so bad they don't feel like themselves anymore. For some people, that comes with neglecting religious duties, for others it's not getting straight As. So the best thing you can do for someone dealing with shame is?"

"To love them!" the room echoes back.

"Exactly! To love them! If your friend is dealing with shame, you hopefully wouldn't want to punch them, you'd want to be there for them. You'd want them to know they're not alone and that you see them for who they really are. It's the same with a loup-garou transformation. If you see someone?"

"Tell someone!" they reply in unison.

Mateo leans in and kisses Gwen on the cheek and she turns her attention away from the assembly. He moves quickly, finding her lips in the dark before she realizes he's trying to make out with her. She puts a hand on his chest to push him away, but he mistakes it for a romantic gesture and puts his hand over hers.

Behind them, their teacher clears her throat loudly, and he sighs, turning his attention back to Mr. Ryan. Gwen exhales, knowing he'll interpret it as shared disappointment and not the relief she feels. She looks out into the sea of faces and spots Roisin looking back at her. Her friend jumps in her seat, surprised, and turns back to watch Mr. Ryan before Gwen can wave to her. Even from across the room, Gwen's surprised at how red her friend's ears seem to have turned.

"Exactly!" he says with forced enthusiasm. "If you see someone, tell someone! Studies show that unreported loups-garous sightings usually lead to a spike of cases, so do your part to prevent outbreaks. Not to mention, as we all know, the only way to stop the loup-garou condition is to recognize the person who's been transformed. So if *you* don't recognize the loup-garou, that doesn't mean someone else won't!"

"Okay, but like, nobody wants to get caught being a loup-garou," the blonde girl says. Although she directs the comment to one of her friends, it's loud enough for the rest of the room to hear. "I think I'd die of embarrassment if someone caught me rutting around the mall with a pig's nose and a curly tail."

From across the room, someone snorts while pretending to ask a store clerk if jeggings are half off. It's not especially funny, but it's enough to send the immature students into hysterics. Mr. Ryan sighs loudly into the mic as the teachers try to get their classes under control.

It's going to be a very long afternoon for all of them.

Mateo runs his hand over the top of Gwen's thigh and her entire body tenses up. When he'd invited her over to "chill", it had been with the understanding that his parents were going to be there too. He'd made it sound like all of them would be spending the afternoon loafing on the couch watching old horror movies and passing around Jiffy Pop popcorn and gummy worms. Instead, she was alone with him in his too-big house and searching for any excuse to leave.

"Uh, this is a really good part," she says, pulling away from him and nodding to the TV. Her hands are balled into fists, which she keeps glued to her sides, and she finds it hard to meet Mateo's gaze.

"Mmm, yeah," he whispers, "this *is* a really good part."

He trails his hand up her thigh a little higher and moves his body even closer to hers, nibbling at her neck. He slips a hand under her shirt, placing it on her stomach, and it feels painfully hot against her skin. The he starts sliding it up.

"Ohmygod, no," she says, pushing him back and leaping to her feet.

"What? Why?"

"I'm not ready."

"What do you mean you're not ready? You seemed like you were totally into this."

"I'm not, I'm really *really* not."

"Babe," he says, looking up at her from his spot on the couch. "Come sit back down. We can take it slower." When she hesitates, he pouts and taps the space next to him. "Please?"

She sits down on the couch, leaving a cushion between then, and tries to focus on the television. But before a full five minutes have passed, he's pressed up against her and kissing a trail up to her ear.

"Okay, no! What did I *literally* just say?" She gets up again and crosses the room, throwing on her jacket and picking up her purse from its spot on the recliner.

"You said you wanted to take it slow! I was taking it slow!"

"Yeah, well now I don't want you taking it anywhere."

"What the hell's your problem? We've been dating for like three months now and we haven't done anything. You don't want to make out with me, you don't want me to touch you, like? Why are you even dating me?"

The question catches her off guard and makes her angry. She's about to say something cruel, but the pained look on his face curbs some of her fury. A long minute goes by before she answers him honestly.

"I just wanted to feel normal. I'm sorry."

Before he can ask any follow-up questions, she heads into the entranceway and pulls on her shoes, before leaving his house and slipping into the night.

At first Gwen thinks it's her imagination acting up, since she hardly slept the night before. Although she tried to squeeze some sleep in before her alarm was set to go off, she spent most of that time awake and worried, trying to imagine how uncomfortable the rest of the semester would be. She only shares two classes with Mateo, but he's a popular guy and has friends in all her other courses, and she can't help but fret that school is suddenly about to get complicated for her. Midterms are behind them, which means finals and (hopefully) college are just around the corner. She doesn't need to worry about her ex-boyfriend, she needs to worry about grades. But when a group of girls from her gym class stops talking just long enough for her to walk by, she knows something's wrong.

People are talking about her.

Eyes follow her as she makes her way down the hall and opens her locker. As she sorts through her books and stores her finished homework in the correct binders, she becomes acutely aware that people aren't just talking about her. They're laughing.

"Have a fun night last night?" a girl asks, a few lockers down.

"Uh, not especially." It's an innocent enough answer, but it elicits cackling from the students listening to the exchange.

"You know, that's exactly what Mateo told us. Well, texted us."

"What do you mean?"

"Don't worry, practice makes perfect." For some reason they also find this hilarious, and they take off down the hall.

Gwen holds her binder and textbook in one arm, shoves her backpack into the locker, and closes it loudly before heading off to her first class. People continue to stare as she makes her way to World History, and more than one student asks if she'd "like to practice" with them. With every "no", and with increased bewilderment from Gwen, the joke gets funnier for everyone else, and by the time she's sitting in the back corner of the classroom she's feeling close to tears. It's only when Roisin takes a seat next to her that a wave of relief hits Gwen.

But it's short-lived.

Roisin stares into her notebook, face flushed, and ignores Gwen's greeting. It's only when the teacher comes in and begins the lecture that she finally looks up from her notes and stares dead ahead. Gwen spends most of the hour trying to get her friend's attention, but it goes ignored and unnoticed. When the bell finally rings, Roisin rushes to leave the room, but Gwen grabs her by the arm and pulls her back.

"What the hell?" she practically cries. "Everyone's been treating me like shit all morning, and you don't want to talk to me? Why? What the hell did I do?"

"Mateo," she says drily.

"What? I thought you'd be happy about that. I mean, I know I should have texted you sooner about it, but like—"

"*Why* would *I* be happy about that?"

"Because you hated him, or at least you acted like it. I thought you'd be thrilled we broke up."

Roisin's head snaps up at this comment, finally meeting Gwen's gaze. "You did what now?"

"I broke up with Mateo. Isn't that what you just said you were mad about?"

Roisin bites her lip and looks down at the floor before exhaling hard. "Oh man, no, that's definitely not what I meant. Gwen, there's a rumour going around that, uh, he broke up with you—"

Gwen rolls her eyes and cuts off her friend. "Of course there is. Whatever, I really can't be bothered with—"

"—because you were bad in bed," she finishes.

Gwen's mouth is suddenly dry and her chest hurts. "He said I was bad in bed?"

Roisin's ears get red and she suddenly can't look at Gwen anymore. "So you *did* sleep with him then?"

"I think I'm going to be sick."

Gwen pushes past Roisin, who calls after her, and she rushes back to her locker. She throws her binder in and grabs her backpack, slamming the door behind her. She runs through the halls and makes her way out of the front door, the whispers and laughs following her home.

She sits on the edge of her bed, opening and closing her hands, the long nails biting into her palm each time. When she got home, she threw up in the entranceway of her house, cleaning it up before her parents got in from work. She then spent the rest of the day locked in her bedroom, saying she wanted to be alone and insisting it was just period cramps when her family came to check on her. She couldn't tell them about the rumour going around the school. She couldn't tell them about a lot of things. Eventually, the afternoon faded into the evening, and by the time the sun had fully set she had transformed into her other self. Her hideous self.

Mr. Ryan had told the assembly that wolves had little to do with loups-garous, but her body had clearly missed the memo. Although she'd never quite cleared five feet when human, she now stood almost seven feet tall, her healthy frame made lean by the extra height. The short brown hair that covered her head now trailed down her chest and her back, and darkened her forearms. Her hands grew bony and her knuckles more pronounced, and her short nails had been replaced by long claws. In this form, her clothing didn't fit, so she fashioned herself a makeshift toga from a bedsheet and belt. She ran a hand across her snout, nose long and mouth wide with pointed teeth, and she tried to choke back the bile she felt creeping up the back of her throat as she looked at herself in the mirror. When she'd first turned into a loup-garou months earlier, the transformation had only been a curse. It was just one more thing to feel ashamed of.

Now, thinking of Mateo and the pain she was eager to inflict, she wonders if it could possibly be a gift. Mr. Ryan said the most

79

dangerous thing about her kind is shame. She disagrees. She thinks it's the razor-sharp appendages.

She opens the bedroom window and steps delicately onto the roof, careful to shut the sliding glass quietly behind her. She tiptoes across the shingles, not wanting to wake up the family dog, before making her way onto the nearby tree branch and climbing down the sturdy maple. Her father has always joked that he should cut down that tree to keep her safe from future boyfriends. Who knew he should have cut it down to keep exes safe from her?

She makes her way across the manicured lawn, the wet grass squishing under her bare feet, as her unnaturally long legs help her cross the space faster than she normally would. Although she hates turning into a monster every night, the physical advantages that come with it are plenty. Her gym class is an exercise in exhaustion and physical ineptitude, but in her loup-garou form she has boundless energy and stamina. It's what normally keeps her up all night, and it's what propels her forward now. She sprints down the dimly lit streets, hoping people are asleep and can't see her, or are too tired to notice or care. The last thing she needs now is for someone to spot her and for her whole school to find out she's a beast.

As she approaches the fence around Mateo's house, her stomach churns and her skin feels hot with betrayal. She knows she hurt him, made him feel unwanted, but what he did? Unforgivable. Cruel. The way they'd all laughed at her. The way they'd all spoken about her.

The way Roisin had looked at her.

Just the thought of it makes her want to shred Mateo to ribbons.

She hopes her ex is good at reading expressions, since loups-garous are notoriously mute, but she thinks she'd be willing to write her grievances in his flesh if push came to shove.

As she stands outside the fence, she hears rustling behind her. At first, Gwen thinks it's an animal, but then the steps get louder and she realizes she's not alone. She turns on her heel, caught off guard, and finds another loup-garou behind her in the grass. The creature is taller than her and sports a long wiry tail. The fur that covers its face is copper and shines like fire under the light of the moon. The creature's bright green eyes widen in surprise, and it lets out a little gasp.

Roisin?

Gwen? The girls think simultaneously.

The air around them changes. Whatever fury and violence brought Gwen to Mateo's yard is released suddenly, like air rushing from a balloon. The two of them stare at each other, transfixed, as the hair vanishes, their bones shorten, and their claws retract. The transformation is over in a matter of seconds, and two barefoot girls wrapped in bedsheets stand where the monsters once stood.

"What the hell are you doing here?" Roisin asks.

"Me? What the hell are *you* doing here? And you're a loup-garou? Since when? Why didn't you tell me?"

"Asked pot to kettle," she snaps. "You first!"

"Okay, uh, well, I was here to kick Mateo's ass."

"Really?"

"Yeah. Maybe more," Gwen admits, pulling the blanket tight around her shoulders. "I was pissed! He lied to the school. We never, you know…"

"I know."

"You do?"

Roisin stares at the ground and runs a hand through her hair. "After you left, I spoke to hi—"

"Spoke?"

She smiles sheepishly. "Okay, I screamed at him. He told me what happened, that he was pissed, and that he made everything up. And when he refused to tell everyone the truth…I don't know. I thought maybe I could intimidate him into admitting he lied."

"You were going to do that for me?"

Roisin shrugs. "Yeah, of course. I'd do anything for you," she says, with a blush.

"Why didn't you tell me you were a loup-garou?" Gwen asks.

"I don't know. I guess I didn't want to ruin our friendship," she admits.

"You thought I'd stop being your friend if you told me you were a loup-garou?"

"No, of course not! It's just…it's complicated."

"Have you been one for long?"

"A year," she says, looking around the empty yard. "I take it this is a new experience for you, courtesy of Mateo?"

Gwen shakes her head, finding it hard to look Roisin in the eyes. "A couple of months."

"What?" she cries. "Why didn't you tell me?"

"I don't know. I guess for the same reason you didn't want to tell me."

With one last look behind her, Gwen turns away from Mateo's house and heads back the way she came, Roisin walking beside her.

"I can't believe you recognized me," Gwen admits, shivering in the cold air.

"I'd know your moody stance anywhere. I'm actually surprised you could tell who I was with those whiskers."

"You mean those ginger whiskers?" she laughs, reaching out to tuck a lock of Roisin's hair behind her ear. "You could shave your head and I'd still recognize that melon."

The two of them chuckle under the moon as they make their way through the maze of quiet streets.

"So what's the big secret?" Roisin asks eventually, as Gwen's house comes into view.

"Oh, uh, maybe let's save that for another night?"

"Mr. Ryan says if you don't spill the beans after someone recognizes you, then the shame will just turn you back again."

"The only thing to fear is shame itself," Gwen imitates.

"Exactly. Might as well rip this band-aid off while we're here."

"Only if you say yours too."

The two of them stand close to each other under a streetlamp, shivering from the cold and their nerves. Gwen's stomach does backflips while Roisin plays compulsively with her hair.

"Same time?" Roisin suggests.

Gwen nods.

"One," says Roisin.

"Two," continues Gwen.

"Three."

"I have a crush on you," they say in unison.

The silence between them grows and expands. At first it feels like it's going to consume them both, but then, just as suddenly, it's gone. Relief and disbelief floods them, and before they know it they're laughing together in the starlight.

"I don't know if I should be happy or terrified," Roisin admits.

"Both. Definitely both."

"So then did you, uh, I don't know, want to hang out or something?" she asks, shifting her weight back and forth on her feet, the pavement rough under her smooth skin.

"We hang out all the time. Take me on a date," Gwen says sheepishly.

Roisin closes the distance between them and pecks Gwen on the cheek, a smile growing on her face as she pulls away. "I'll see what I can do."

"Get home safe," she says.

Roisin waves a shy farewell and Gwen watches her walk away into the night, staring into the distance long after she's faded from view.

As she heads back to her house, she can't help but chuckle. Maybe Mr. Ryan was right after all.

CAITLIN MARCEAU is an author and lecturer living and working in Montreal. She holds a B.A. in Creative Writing, is a member of both the Horror Writers Association and the Quebec Writers 'Federation, and spends most of her time writing horror and experimental fiction. She's been published for journalism and poetry, as well as creative non-fiction, and has spoken about horror literature at several Canadian conventions. Her collections, A Blackness Absolute *and* Palimpsest, *are slated for publication by D&T Publishing LLC and Ghost Orchid Press in 2022, respectively. If she's not covered in ink or wading through stacks of paper, you can find her ranting about issues in pop culture or nerding out over a good book. For more, check out CaitlinMarceau.ca.*

RESIN

Amanda M. Blake

"Lillian, do you see her?"

"See who? Mrs. Milner across the street?"

Rose pointed through the glass. "No. Look."

Mom and Dad had chosen to move us into a neighborhood that felt lived-in, with trees as tall as those in the forested area we'd left, because they thought shade would make us feel more at home.

The tree in the side yard that comprised Rose's primary view must have stood there for fifty years, maybe longer. The base of the trunk could nestle two people within, and it split up to densely leaved branches that muraled both windows in Rose's bedroom. From the angle she tucked herself in her window seat, the knots and growths in the trunk, where the closest branch split away, looked just like the body of a woman stretching luxuriously toward the deciduous canopy above.

The knots that made up the breasts were barked, except for the centers, which were lipped and smooth. The grain of the bark then arrowed down what seemed like a waist, to the juncture of living branch and trunk, where another smooth knot had formed, with an unmistakable cleft in the center.

Knots form where branches are broken or cut away. The expanding rings of the trunk grow over the wound. They're also weak points—tough to cut through but less sound, which is why they crack in cross-sections. There was nothing particularly unusual about how the tree had scarred over its amputations. The shape of its scars was pure pareidolic, pornographic coincidence, a mature figure for a mature tree.

"You've got to be kidding me." I couldn't help but laugh, although it made me uncomfortable, like looking at a dirty Polaroid pic of someone I knew, or maybe myself in five years. It was unsettlingly adult, the way some of my feelings could be at the most inopportune and overwhelming times.

"I know." Rose rested her head against the windowpane again, tucking her hair behind her ears. The longer it grew, the more she didn't know how to get it out of the way, because it was still too short for a rubber band. She couldn't quite meet my eyes. "You won't tell Mom and Dad, right?"

Our parents told us that we moved from our small town to the suburbs because they needed a change of pace, but really, it was because small towns have a way of becoming smaller. Once something's known, it can't be unknown, even if what people know is incomplete or some lurid backroom version of what actually happened.

Jessica's parents couldn't afford to move away from all that. She was still back there, alone, with her whole world staring at her and seeing something else. Jessica didn't have an escape; Rose hadn't wanted to escape in the first place. Mom and Dad had dragged her out of our hometown kicking and screaming—figuratively speaking, because she'd been eerily silent the whole trip, blank, absent, almost dead. And whenever Mom or Dad called her down for dinner now, she maintained that same silence—eerie because it was neither petulant nor punishment.

Our parents thought it was, though, because after the first week of silent treatment, they banned her from the living room computer except for homework, so Dad could watch over her shoulder. I'd often peeked into her bedroom when she'd curled up on the bed crying those first few weeks, but after she stopped crying, if I hadn't seen her breathing, I might have called an ambulance—or a funeral home.

The way she now looked out the window at the woman in the tree wasn't with the same light I remembered from when she and Jessica had hung out together during or after school, but there was at least some kind of life—like the movement of jellyfish tentacles instead of a plastic grocery bag in the ocean. I wasn't sure whether I preferred it.

Mom and Dad never looked out the window themselves to see what enthralled her, but they did notice when she missed Wednesday night youth group and choir rehearsal at the church. And they noticed when she didn't wear the clothes Mom laid out for her. And they noticed when she chopped her hair off with the kitchen scissors while Mom and Dad were asleep. And they definitely noticed when—emboldened by the fact that our parents hadn't punished her for those little defiances to the rules they'd discussed with her before the move—she crept downstairs to call Jessica. Jessica's mom answered and refused to let Rose talk to her daughter, then Mom got a phone call of her own the next morning.

With grim masks, she and Dad moved the landline from the kitchen to the main bedroom. Dad drove to the bookstore and returned with an armful of hardline hardbacks and paperbacks with confused teenagers or ominously gender-ambiguous bracelets on the front cover. A Bible verse preceded every book description, and solemn men and women emoted compassion under every author biography. He set them on a shelf in the living room, and he and Mom read through them, one by one, every night after Rose and I were supposed to be in bed or doing homework.

After they'd pored through the whole shelf, they sat down with Rose to carve the boundaries deeper. I wasn't invited to that party, but I heard my parents talking in low, security-guard tones and Rose not talking at all. I got the gist of the song, though, because the melody kept playing in the weeks to come.

"It's not hard to lie. We do it all the time. Why don't you just fake it until you can move out of the house?" I asked, after Mom had taken her to the salon so her hair wouldn't look as jagged or boyish as before. Rose was wearing makeup, too. Mom made sure she left the house every day with all the basics—lipstick or lip gloss, blush, mascara, eyeshadow. She could keep a tube of lip gloss in her purse or her backpack to touch up, but Mom expected the rest to still be on Rose's face when she got home. She could only take it off at night before bed.

"What do you think they're trying to get me to do?" Earrings dangled from ears that had been pierced for Rose's tenth birthday. They'd kept almost closing because she wouldn't wear anything in them, but now Mom included accessories next to the mandatory clothes and makeup she set out for her daughter.

"It's just for a few more years."

"There's a difference between lying about what you do and lying about who you are. Some people are better at it than others. Look at me. Does it look like I'm good at lying about who I am?"

Mom and Dad had piled every last one of her baggy pants, concert t-shirts, leather bracelets, and bandannas into paper department store bags for donation, until all that remained were clothes that Mom had bought her at back-to-school sales and for Christmas gifts—the ones Rose had always left in the back of her closet or the corner of her dresser with tags and stickers on.

So Mom adorned her eldest daughter in skirts and dresses, bras with bows and lace, earrings and eyeliner, just like she'd always wanted to, but no amount of wishful thinking or tough love could make Rose with a skirt and feathery hair look natural. She might as well have worn a medieval gown and cilice for how awkward they made her seem.

Bus to school and bus back, her hand-me-down car trapped on the driveway because Mom and Dad had taken the keys. If Rose didn't come home on time, Mom swore to drop everything she was doing to look in every ditch on the way to school and shout to the rooftops to mortify Rose when she arrived. If Rose had to stay after school, she was expected to call. Mom would pick her up when her activity—generally a group project in the library—was done, as long as she could vet the other students.

As soon as Rose came home, she went straight to her room, which had been painted dusky pink in her absence one school day. She'd been named Rose at birth and liked it as much as a person can like the name they're given, but she would never in a million years have painted her room pink.

Even so, Rose had no problem spending all of her time there. She would do her homework or read to entertain herself, but every time I passed by and her bedroom door was still open, I found her on the window seat, peering out. She remembered to close the door for some privacy if she wasn't there for the tree, but something about it fogged her mind.

Rose is confused, Dad had explained to me. *We just need to clear up her confusion, like when we go over your math homework.*

But even back then, I knew Rose's issues weren't computation errors. Love and desire were the sloppiest, ugliest things in the world, and they weren't something you decided, or else I would have shut it off entirely myself. Who wants to be thirteen and tripping over words with boys you used to play four-square with? Who wants to be told to focus on school when all you can think about is what's done under covers, even if you have a clearer picture of the math than the sex?

So maybe I understood when I passed by her room that evening, on the way to study, and found her with her hand under her skirt, cheek pressed hard against the glass and eyes hooded. I froze in the hallway, my textbooks in my arms, caught between mortified and morbidly curious.

I hadn't gone that far yet, hadn't figured out how, and the puberty classes I'd taken a few years earlier certainly hadn't cleared any of that up, because the same books Mom and Dad used to try and correct Rose had just as much to say about tending to oneself as they did about tending to the wrong person.

I knew I should leave, knew I wasn't supposed to see this, that no matter what Rose was thinking about in her mind, it didn't matter—it wasn't mine to see. But I couldn't move, a flush moving through me in waves, a disorienting sick swirl.

"What's going on, baby?" Mom slowed on her way up the stairs, taking in the cold-hot guilt crawling under my skin to expose itself on my face. Then she turned onto the landing. Her hand flew to her throat, where she made a sound like she'd been punched in her windpipe. For a moment, she, too, seemed frozen in place.

But only for a moment.

"Rose Amelia Stanton!"

The bedroom door hit the jam and bounced off the spring as Mom stormed in. Rose jerked her hand out from under the skirt and tried to smooth her clothes down, but she couldn't make Mom forget what she'd seen.

"We do *not* do that in this household! And in front of your sister, too. I will not have you corrupt—"

Mom and Dad took the pictures from her walls, the ones of her friends from our hometown, a group of girls and boys here, a group of girls from the soccer team there. They'd already removed all the pictures of Jessica, of course, but now they intended to rid her of every potential temptation. That meant any innocuous picture of another girl, all of Rose's harmless doodles and sketches, as well as any book with a girl on the cover. The air stung with smoke as Mom and Dad stoked the fire in the firepit and said they were doing this for her own good.

And the cruelest cut was that they were, or they thought they were. The books they trusted told them that what Rose was doing was a perversion of godly love, that like any sin, it could be corrected, and as for any teenager, it needed to be corrected with a firm, unflinching hand and barbed-wire borders: *Your kids are looking for guidance. Every time they push back, they're asking you to set the boundary. They may say they hate you, but beyond their naturally sinful nature trying to find a foothold, they love you for loving them enough.*

Just as Mom and Dad had arranged for braces to move and shape my teeth, they shaped Rose with pruning shears, bringing back the silent tears as she watched her memories burn. Then they unscrewed her bedroom door from the hinges.

But even when Mom had barged in and jerked Rose from the window seat, she hadn't happened to look out the window at what Rose had been staring at, any more than she and Dad had noticed it when they'd bought the house for the trees. Without memories to camouflage her pink-painted room, without a door to provide her an older teenager's privacy, and without most of her books, Rose still had the woman in the tree to keep her company.

And although she withdrew from us even more, sometimes she still invited me to join her. I sat in the other window seat while doing my homework, or I squeezed in with her and considered the woman like I would a slab of carved marble in an art gallery, trying not to think of what Rose saw, trying not to imagine anyone looking at me like that. But you know how contrary an imagination is—always thinking of the thing you try so hard not to.

"Do you know what a dryad is?" Rose asked. Our legs overlapped between us on the cushion.

"Sounds like a dryer sheet."

Rose snorted. "It's a type of nymph. Do you know what that is?"

"A girl who has as much sex as the boy who's having it with her?"

"Good girl." Rose ruffled my hair, herself for a fraction of a moment, before turning back to the tree. "A nymph is a type of Greek goddess or fairy who lives in natural things. A naiad is a river nymph. A dryad is a tree nymph."

"And you think a Greek goddess is living in a Texas tree?"

She squinted out at the woman, peering through the deepening dusk. "What's that?"

"Apparently a dryad. Haven't you been paying attention?"

She hit my leg. "No, you goober. Get up."

I climbed off the window seat as she scooted to her knees and flipped the levers on the window to open it.

"What the hell are you doing?" I glanced behind me, hoping our parents hadn't heard and assumed she was trying to run away.

Rose climbed onto the roof, wincing at the sandpapery texture of the shingles on her feet as well as the incline, which seemed so much steeper when someone was on it. She crab-crawled down to the juncture of the branch and straddled it, her skirt draping down over both sides. Then she reached out to touch the woman's belly, just above the tiniest knot that could have been a navel. When she pulled her hand away, strings of some kind of fluid stretched between her fingers and the bark.

She held her hand closer to her face and sniffed. "I think it's tree sap."

"Well, don't touch it!"

"It's not dangerous. They make maple syrup from tree sap."

"Yeah, from maples. Does this look like Canada?"

"We have maples here, Lills."

"Okay, does this look like a maple to you? Oh my God, don't put that in your mouth. You don't know where it's been."

"Sure I do. Inside the tree." She sucked the sap on her fingertips like spilled honey.

"Well? Is it poison? Is it hemlock? Are you dead?"

Rose lingered on one of her fingers, a film passing over her eyes as though she saw something in front of her that wasn't there, as though *she* wasn't entirely there anymore. "It's not maple syrup, but it's still...sweet."

"Rose, get back up here."

95

"Okay, okay, scaredy-cat. It's dripping everywhere over here, though. She's all shiny."

"Seriously, what am I going to tell Mom and Dad if you keel over into the side yard because you put something in your mouth that you shouldn't have?"

"What else would be new?" she said dryly as she climbed back in.

I sighed with relief when she finally stood on solid bedroom carpet, but as I left, she was idly tasting her fingertips again.

After that, she stopped joining us for dinner. When she got home from school, she went straight to her room, then didn't come down until school the next day. On Sundays, Mom forced her to go to church with us, but she'd run right back up to her bedroom afterward.

If we ate out after church, I wasn't wholly certain she ate a bit of her meal, so much as rearranged it on the plate.

Mom and Dad considered her behavior nothing more than normal teenage rebellion, the adolescent version of holding her breath. They figured that, after her cheeks got beet red and she started to shake, Rose would eventually have to let it out. She had lunch at school—although Mom and Dad didn't seem to notice that I brought home my lunch money envelope to replenish the account, and Rose didn't—and they didn't mind if she foraged in the fridge at night, only if she called someone she shouldn't. But I was the only one grabbing a midnight snack or two, because I was hungry all the time and couldn't figure out how Rose went three hours without eating, much less a weekend.

Her skin slipped on her frame, and her clothes became as loose as she preferred them, although the clothes hadn't been designed for it.

I expressed my concerns to Mom and Dad first, because if they could force her to do things to save her soul, surely they could force her to do things to save her life, but Mom patted my back in reassurance. *She'll eat when she's ready.*

Three weeks. People weren't supposed to last that long without eating, even if they drank water, and I didn't see Rose drinking either.

Three weeks of Rose rushing through homework—or sleepwalking through it, if Mom's lecture two weeks in was any indication—so that she could tuck herself back in the window, sometimes in her school clothes, sometimes already in her pink, lacy nightgown, and sometimes just in her underwear as though she still had a door hinged to the frame.

Three weeks of Rose barely acknowledging me and not seeming to see Mom and Dad at all. She didn't throw me out of her room when I went in there to do my homework with her, but when I asked questions, she didn't respond, and I had the disorienting sense that I was the only one still in the room.

Three weeks of showers and laundry at two in the morning. Three weeks of dirty fingernails.

I felt queasy all the time—thinking about Rose, worrying about Rose, worried that I knew what was happening and refusing to let myself understand—but just like Mom and Dad continued to maintain their usual routine, I had to as well. I kept expecting everything to stop, for *someone* to notice how bad things were, because someone or something *should* stop when a girl was so clearly sick. This wasn't moodiness; this wasn't even grief.

Something was wrong with Rose and no one cared, because at least she wasn't being a lesbian anymore.

On Friday night, I decided I wanted popcorn and a movie after Mom and Dad had gone to bed. I stayed up until after midnight with the volume on low, then climbed the stairs.

Rose had her bedside lamp on, a lantern in the dark casting strange shapes on impersonal pink walls. Her bed was unmade but unslept in, and she was in neither of her window seats, but her preferred cushion was askew, the window cracked open.

She hadn't come down while I'd been in the living room. I would have heard the fridge if she'd opened it. But other than my room, which was dark, and the bathroom, which was empty, there was nowhere else she could have been.

"Rose?"

The closet was still full and it didn't look like she'd taken anything with her, but there was no reason why she would have. Mom and Dad had already given away or burned anything of value to her, stripped her away until she fit some comic-book version of what a girl was supposed to be—and I could see so clearly how bullshit it was, because they'd never taken away my jeans or my girl-protagonist novels or the pictures of me with my friends peppering my bedroom walls.

Rose is confused, honey, Dad had repeated when I'd brought it up. *You're not.*

Rose and Jessica had been caught in the school auditorium doing what they'd been doing with determined conviction, while my tongue tied up in knots every time a boy I liked looked in my direction. I knew which one of us was confused, and it wasn't the daughter on whom they'd fixed all their righteous fixer-upper energy.

"Rose?" As though she were hiding under the bed or behind the frame of her open closet. As though she hadn't finally just said 'screw it' and decided to take her chances on streets that would take her more honestly than this comfortable, shaded dollhouse. I'd been there when she'd learned she could crawl from the window, and although the tree wasn't ideal for climbing, the branch just off the roof would at least make it easier to drop down without breaking her leg.

I knelt on the seat and opened the window more than a crack to see beyond the reflection of light. Because of that light, even dim, it took me a minute to really realize what I was seeing in the shifting shadows.

Rose draped over the branch that led to the woman's shape in the tree. The lamplight was just enough to illuminate the full torso that had formed in the tree trunk, because she gleamed with still more tree sap, thick now like smoothed skin over the bark, feminine shape all the more apparent without the roughness. Rose hungrily buried her mouth at the base, where the dripping sap built up like honey at the cleft knot where branch met trunk.

She was silent, or at least quiet enough that I couldn't hear her, but the hand that didn't hold her to the trunk moved furiously, insinuated between her thighs.

The lower half of her face gleamed like the woman's body from where sap had smeared, but so did her cheeks and her eyelashes from tears, thinner and with an easier shine than what seeped from the tree.

"Rosie…" But I might not have said anything, only thought it, and Rose wouldn't have noticed a tornado, much less a whisper in the dark. Her entire world had narrowed to consuming as much as she could from what the tree offered, as though that was all she'd eaten this whole time.

I often experienced arousal mixed with discomfort and even fear at that time in my life—from the power of it, from the thick, dark mist roiling in my mind and sinking to swirl low in my abdomen, from the waves and eddies of desire that I couldn't control and that threatened to drown me if I couldn't tangle my fingers into fists and hold them down, which was like clenching storm clouds. Although I'd known that Rose and I had been brought here because of sex, it was another thing to witness so plainly what my sister wanted and how helpless she was to it, as helpless to its raging as I was to mine.

I covered my mouth against the flush of nausea in my face and in my stomach, against the swell of desire for desire itself, despite my profound embarrassment at catching her—again—but this time when she was doing something so much more intimate, so much more private, although she'd been stripped of all of her privacy.

This wasn't right. It wasn't right that she was finding sex and satiation from a woman shape in a tree outside her bedroom window in the absence of everything else, wasn't right that it had taken over her every spare waking moment, wasn't right that everything else had faded away, including Rose herself, and that she only came alive with tree sap sliding slowly down her throat. It wasn't right that I couldn't run downstairs and tell our parents what was happening, because I was afraid what they would do next, afraid what someone sawing down the tree and throwing it piece by piece into a woodchipper would do to Rose when that tree was the very last thing she had left.

I should have told someone. Something was too wrong with what was happening to her for me to leave it alone. But I kept my mouth covered and backed out of the bedroom, trying to unsee what I'd seen, with about as much success as you'd expect.

It wasn't until Sunday morning that we realized she still wasn't in her bedroom.

That was when we found her in golden morning daylight, emaciated, distorted, straddling the branch and embracing the woman, flush against her, body to body, and encased in hardening resin. She held herself against the woman and smiled: a Rose in amber.

AMANDA M. BLAKE *is a cat-loving daydreamer and mid-age goth who loves geekery of all sorts, from superheroes to horror movies, urban fantasy to unconventional romance. She's the author of horror titles such as* Nocturne *and* Deep Down, *and the fairy tale mash-up series,* Thorns.

Twitter: twitter.com/AmandaMBlake1
FB: facebook.com/authoramandamblake
Instagram: instagram.com/amanda_mblake
Website: amandamblake.com

THE PERFECT MAN

Felix Foote

This wasn't the first time I had chased someone away.

Elias and I first met through our theater classes. From the first moment I saw him, I was entranced. He was already the man of my dreams through appearance alone, with thick, silky, curling hair, warm brown eyes, a kind smile, and a large, cuddly body. He wowed me further with his gorgeous singing voice, almost like an opera singer's, and with a charisma that was as natural to him as breathing. Even his laughter was music to me. When I made that laugh ring through a room like a bright church bell, I was the happiest man in the world. For a few months, we were close friends, and growing closer every day.

Even after I learned he had a boyfriend, that didn't stop me from trying to make Elias happy whenever we were together. I adored him, but all I needed was to have him in my life, smiling that beautiful smile of his.

That was all I wanted.

But it couldn't last. Before I knew it, the smiles he gave in response to my jokes were fake. Not only would he decline any offer to hang out with me, he avoided socializing with people after classes alto-gether. I tried to survive on denial for as long as I could, but it took seeing him dart around a corner to avoid me to finally accept that I had somehow ruined another relationship.

And so, I processed my newly broken heart in the only way that I, or any reasonable man, could.

I made a statue of Elias.

One day, I found one of my classmates lugging a huge box from our university's pottery class to the trashcans. The box was filled with clay—big, wet bricks of it. It was the largest amount of fresh, unused clay that I had ever seen in one place.

It seemed like a waste to throw all that out, and I said as much. My classmate agreed with me, but explained that the professor had in-sisted her class shouldn't use the clay. Apparently, she learned some-thing bad about where it came from after she ordered it, and it couldn't be returned.

I convinced my friend to let me take the clay. My original plan was to resell it. I was a starving college student, after all. I had to eat some-how.

On the way home, I had another idea. At first, it was too ridiculous to recognize how disturbing it was. But the idea kept growing in my mind, molding itself into something bigger with each step to my dorm room. Once I was there, I immediately found some old newspaper to cover a section of the floor.

I reached into the box and grabbed the first block of clay. The mo-ment my hands sunk into its thick, earthen surface, I knew there was no going back. I worked through the night with no breaks, not even to use the bathroom. My hands were clumsy, but quick. The more I handled the clay, the more determined I became. It was only when the box of clay was empty, and the sun started peeking through the clouds, that I let myself sit back and truly admire my handiwork.

My clay man was born.

Miraculously, there was just enough clay to make a figure about as tall as Elias. I managed to achieve the shape of his soft stomach, and the statue's proportions were only slightly inhuman. However, I had neither the leftover clay nor the expertise to make Elias's curly hair, so the top of the clay man's head remained a bald, misshapen, fingerprint-covered dome.

Any attempts to add details to its eyes were laughably hideous, so they too remained smooth and blank.

I was also bothered by its lack of lips. Elias's were plush and curved in a lovely way, lips that anyone would dream of kissing.

My clay man's grin was a lopsided line.

And yet, somehow, it comforted me. Perhaps it was just my heartbroken mind desperately convincing itself that those hours of sculpting were worth it, and that this was a totally reasonable way of coping with rejection. Even so, it was nice to have a friendly presence in my room. Someone to turn to when I felt alone.

I started talking to it. I didn't think of it as Elias—it was too grotesque for that—but I talked to it in the way I used to talk to him. I would perform the jokes that Elias wouldn't listen to anymore. I would tell it about my day, my classes, anything that was on my mind.

I would also talk about Elias. I didn't want to badmouth my one source of comfort, but sometimes, I would wish the clay man had Elias's best features.

"If only you had his hair," I said, "you'd be perfect."

"If only you had his eyes, you'd be perfect."

"If only you had his lips, you'd be perfect."

One night, in a rush of desperation, I placed my hands on the statue's shoulders and kissed the clay man on its lipless mouth.

The experience immediately sobered me up. The clay was dry and earthy, and the kiss left me rubbing my mouth on my sleeve. I meekly returned to my normal routine.

That night was the last normal night of my life.

After that kiss, my nights were filled with strange noises. The same noise repeated every night, and my dreams began to revolve around it. It was a long, slow, shuffling sound. The sound you would hear when dragging furniture around a carpeted space, or when you dragged your feet while walking very slowly.

What worried me more was the sudden presence of dust in my bed-sheets. I felt it when I woke up, rubbing against my bare skin. At first, I wasn't surprised. Most of the floor had become coated in dust and dried clay segments the size of grains of sand, even though my clay man remained in his corner of the room. It wasn't a stretch to think that I had brought this detritus with me from the bottoms of my feet. Then I remembered that I always wore slippers around my room, which I would take off before climbing into bed.

Still, I ignored the noises in the middle of the night, and the tracks of clay dust that collected on the path from the corner of the room to my bedside.

One day, Elias and I had an argument after class. In short, I had asked Elias if he wanted to hang out while lightly suggesting that he could not bring his boyfriend along. This resulted in a fight that left me sobbing all the way home, and pouring my broken heart out to the clay man. At one point, I draped myself over the statue, sobbing into the nape of its neck.

Just before I finished crying, with my heart no less broken, I said, "I wish you could help me. Then...."

I wondered whether to say "I would be fine," or "I wouldn't be alone." But somehow, what came out was,

"You'd be perfect."

As I drifted off to sleep that night, the shuffling noises happened again. This time, my dreams were different. I've had sleep paralysis in the past, and have even seen things during it, so when I opened my eyes and saw a figure draped in shadows standing by my bed, I didn't panic.

I was only unsettled when my gaze wandered to the corner of my room, or as much of it as I could see in the dark. It almost looked like it was empty—as if the statue was gone. I fell back into unconsciousness, and when I awoke the next morning, the clay man was waiting in its corner.

I spent the day at the biggest art museum in the city to cheer me up from the previous day's fight, but to no avail. I could barely focus on any painting, and seeing the statues only made me blush. Disheartened, I caught the train home.

Once I'd taken my seat, I checked the time on my phone. Suddenly, a notification popped up.

A message from Elias.

Just as white-hot panic started burning in my chest, the notification disappeared. Puzzled, I opened the Messenger app. It had been a while since I last sent Elias a message, but I certainly didn't remember seeing the most recent messages on my screen. The timestamps even said that most of them were from today.

My panic returned when another message appeared.

A message from me.

Someone had access to my account.

Before I could type a warning, I lost the signal. My subway ride home was underground, and I could only connect to 4G when the train was in a station. I took this time to read the previous messages.

Whoever was controlling my account had initiated the conversation with a simple, *"We need to talk."*

After a few minutes, Elias had responded, *"I think we should."*

The anxiety clawing at me never fully stopped, but it did soothe somewhat when I saw the conversation hadn't played out that badly. My account's hijacker apologized for I had done, recognizing that it had been out of line. They stated calmly that I had meant no harm, but that I can lose sight of how to act when I become enamored with somebody. I had only planned to enjoy Elias's company as my friend, and

I still wished for this to happen. Honestly, this was better than anything I could have written myself.

But this only proved the existence of a new problem: how did they know all this? How did a stranger know all of this information, which I hadn't shared with another soul?

The train pulled into a station and the 4G returned. I prepared to type that my account had been compromised, but paused when I read Elias's response to the "confession".

"I'm relieved you said all that," he wrote. *"I regretted blowing up at you yesterday from the moment I started yelling. You're a cool person, but your crush on me has been super obvious. I've been telling my boyfriend about all this, and it's caused some arguments between us. I took out all that frustration on you. Even with the way you've been acting, that wasn't fair. I'm really sorry."*

I listened to the train doors open and close in front of me as I slowly started to smile. The grimy subway fell away as I learned that Elias didn't hate me. My heart, my soul, my entire life, was filled with hope.

Then the next message from my hijacker arrived.

"Let's apologize for real. Meet me at my dorm room."

I almost dropped my phone in an attempt to interject, but it was too late. The train had left the station. I was offline again.

Fortunately, the next stop was mine. I tried to calm my racing mind with the plan that I would leave the train, find a bench, and salvage the situation as much as I could. I couldn't stop thinking about what this hijacker was planning. He didn't really know where my dorm room was, did he? How could I doubt him if he knew so many of my other secrets?

What did he want with Elias?

Finally, my phone dinged. The train was just pulling into the station.

"A face-to-face convo would do us good," Elias had replied. *"I'm actually not far from your dorm room now."*

"Good," said my hijacker. *"I can't wait to fix things."*

Those messages were from five minutes ago.

The newest message from Elias said, *"I'm here."*

The train doors opened.

"Come upstairs. Then everything will be perfect."

I ran.

Any thought of warning Elias was gone. It was too late now. I bumped into a lot of strangers on the sprint back to the dorms, but I didn't care. I needed to make sure Elias was okay.

I stopped running only after I had leapt up the stairs to my dorm room's floor. I was exhausted, but what really stopped me were the stains. The dark, red stains.

Underneath a new indentation on the wall opposite my door—as if something had hit it with considerable force—a trail of blood stretched over the filthy carpet to my room.

I should have called the police. I should have called the R.A. I should have run and never looked back.

Instead, I took the expired fire extinguisher from its spot next to the stairwell and braced myself as I tried to open the door. I always locked my dorm room before going outside, and kept the key on a lanyard around my neck. I felt sick at how the unlocked door swung open.

By now, it was night-time. The only sources of illumination were the lights from the hallway, the meager moonlight coming through the window, and my open laptop. My room isn't very large. Even though my laptop was at the far end of it, I could still interpret the layout of Facebook and the shape of the Messenger chat box.

There was a figure standing in the middle of the room, far enough from the hallway's light to be in shadows. I recognized the proportions of his body, and the messy curls on his head. It was Elias!

I started to run, but my feet caught on something large that was sprawled on the floor. I dropped my makeshift weapon as I fell on top of it. My mouth, which had opened to call out to Elias, tasted blood.

I had been so focused on the figure standing before me, so tired from my panicked run, that I had missed the man lying on the floor. He was partly hidden by shadows, but now I could see him clearly.

His head was so disfigured that I couldn't call him human. Some-thing had imperfectly ripped his scalp from his skull. Spots of white peeked out from the mass of oozing red. His eyes were replaced by empty wet sockets. His mouth was open in an abandoned final scream, but without any lips to frame it. These horrifying absences combined to form the link between a bare skull and a human head: a pile of bone, tissue, and blood.

Although the dead man's face was unrecognizable, his body and the style of his clothes told me exactly who he was. I did nothing to stop the scream that escaped me.

My poor Elias.

The standing figure finally stepped into the light. Now I could see the blood dripping from the borrowed hair on its head, the burst and runny sacks leaking from sockets it must have physically carved into its own head, and the bits of flayed flesh that framed its mouth.

My clay man stepped forward, powder spilling from every bend of its cracked limbs. Its mouth opened, and a low dry voice came out. What it said rang in my ears as it grabbed me and crushed its face against mine in a crude performance of a kiss.

"Now, I'm perfect."

FELIX FOOTE was born and bred in Manhattan, and is probably the most mild-mannered New Yorker who has ever lived. He earned his BA in Creative Writing at Bard College at Simon's Rock. As he works on his prose fiction, he also regularly updates his original weekly webcomic, The Antics of Softboy Pillowman, *which you can find at softboy-pillowman.tumblr.com. He's also on Twitter @felixthe-scholar.*

AFTER THE FLOOD
Monica Robinson

The storm hit earlier than the weatherman predicted, and Alex was caught in a heavy sheet of rain as she pulled her car out of the lot. She was leaving work and heading to her apartment, weaving through city traffic and the downpour both. Wind whipped the trees against the hapless power lines, and drivers slowed for the puddles that dredged and drowned the road, headlights barely denting the thick, grey clouds that lingered too close to the low horizon.

The chaos of the storm lit the blood in Alex's veins like a lightning strike. The bass of her music crashed over the car speakers as she splashed recklessly through the water that gathered on the roadside banks and wove between other drivers, eager with the energy of the storm and familiar with each curve of the road, even as the lanes shifted to avoid orange cones and construction, abandoned in the downpour. Rain washed over the piles of rocky silt left behind, filling the gaping holes awaiting sidewalks with pools of water that threatened to spill over. When it rained in these old East Coast cities, the infrastructure rejected it, the ground refused to absorb it, and the water

113

rose swift and relentless, rushing past in the sunken grass alongside the road in sudden rivers.

Alex watched, chaos-ridden grin on her face, as lightning forked across a tumultuous, angry sky, as thunder tumbled along to the recurring stereo bass, and as an ancient, electrifying blood coursed through her veins. There was little she loved more than a truly vivacious storm—restless, ceaseless, and unforgiving.

By the time she arrived in her own parking lot (a rarity, in the city, but one she was thankful for nonetheless, though occasionally she forgot to be grateful when she came home late and found the lot full and was forced to try her luck on the surrounding streets), a handful of downed branches littered the asphalt and the sky had shifted from grey to a sick, greenish hue—nature's warning that she recognized so well from a lifetime of living in the Midwest. It was strange to see it here, with the nearby curve of those ancient and unmoving mountains dividing the flat-land states from those bordering the coast. Still, she was in no hurry to rush inside in spite of it.

The pull of the wind and the hallowed rush of the rain drew her in, a siren's call from the heavens that lured her out into the vast, roaring expanse of the angry sky. She had found her way to the apartment in her heretical storm daze, and was immediately greeted by the wafting, homely scent of warm food on the stove, the weather playing loudly in the background on the mounted TV, her brother's car-grease shoes placed deliberately on the mat by the door.

They seldom cooked true meals, either of them, but when the weather was right and his mood was amiable, and when he had the time, Cal would throw together that easy one-pot stew they both loved and they would watch old horror movies over bowls of it, fingers wrapped around to sap the heat.

Alex announced her presence half-heartedly, distracted by the weather map on the TV, the reach of the storms much wider than she had anticipated. She was not worried, so much as she felt a tinge of guilt at her enjoyment of such destruction, though she had not realized its breadth as she'd been driving. Cal called something back in response, but she didn't register it as she watched three confirmed tornadoes mapped across their twenty-mile radius.

"Have you seen this?" she asked, in the general direction of the kitchen.

"Yeah—we'll go down to the laundry room if it gets worse," Cade responded, stoic.

She shed her jacket, shoes, and bag in a trail behind her, tired and absent-minded. Or rather, single-minded, as she turned the corner into the kitchen, following the smell and the warm familiarity of Cal's voice. The day had been long and dull and the customers had been rude—she was tired of day jobs and the city, or, more accurately, being in the midst of it and serving rude customers all day. She had an essay due, thirty pages of reading before her next class, and a million other things to do on top of that, but for a moment she reveled in the stillness of the space, the warmth of the kitchen and the delicious smell of a dinner home-cooked for her, and she let it be enough in that moment.

She only realized that she had zoned out when she became aware of Cal's fingers snapping in front of her face, his teasing "You good?" that contained the faintest hint of worry.

She grinned widely back at him. "I'm fine. Just . . . fine."

They ate soup. They watched their warped VHS copy of *Nightmare on Elm Street*, and they kept one eye each on the weather. Alex, exhausted, pressed through her homework, and Cal, beside her, soldered something together, though she wasn't sure what exactly it was, only that sparks jumped worryingly from between his calloused hands from time to time. She fell asleep that night to a steady pounding of rain and the distinct summer sound that followed, nestled in the thick of her comforter with the fan spinning cool air overhead.

Her sleep was interrupted around 2 a.m., though at first she awoke drowsy and confused and could not place what had woken her. The rain still pattered against the window pane, but it was slower and softer, and when she strained for the sound of thunder, she did not hear it. It was then that the realization of what had awoken her hit—a door opening. Which door, she could not say, and so she found herself creeping out of her cocoon of a bed with a Bowie knife cradled in one hand, gingerly, as though she was afraid she might actually need to use it.

The living room was still and silent, dark save for the flicker of the TV's power button. The front door appeared untouched and, once her eyes adjusted to the light, she realized the door to the balcony was cracked ever so slightly, the faint glow of a lit cigarette illuminating the deeply shadowed face of Cal sitting hunched over in one of the chairs.

As she moved closer, she could see that he was shirtless and sleep-tousled, startled awake from the depths of sleep by . . . something. The storm, or something else. Though his back was to her, he had evidently heard her hesitant steps over the threshold, the subtle creak of the hinges on the door, because without turning his head, he spoke to her in a voice thick with fatigue: "Don't you dare take up smoking. This is not an example."

She didn't respond, but took his speech as an invitation to sit in the chair next to him, curled with her feet up like a cat, reflective eyes and all. For a moment, the only sounds were the soft pattering of the rain, the crackle of the cigarette as the end burnt with each slow inhale, and the very faint clap of thunder in the distance. The storm had moved on, but when Alex looked down from their third-floor balcony, she could see the river swollen well over its banks. Main Street flooded with a rush of water, carrying with it parking barriers and pieces of gates and whole doors ripped from rusted hinges, passing like mon-strous water-dwellers in the darkness below. The water covered the roads in and out, the parking lot below, rising to the tops of the cars. She could see her Jeep just barely above the wavering surface.

In the distance, sirens broke through the rain and stillness that stretched across the early hours. Somewhere on the horizon, dawn threatened to rise but had not, yet.

There were no more words passed between them as they observed the chaos, the flooded cars still undiscovered, and the far, destructive reach of the angry river. There was little to say that entirely encompassed the scene below. Alex couldn't conceptualize the future, tomorrow, only that moment on the balcony side by side, as the wind stirred around them and Cal stared out into the distance, guiltily lighting cigarette after cigarette as though the smoke mattered with the weight of the water resulted in a phantom pressure on his chest as he met its unending, dark-eyed gaze.

It was never an option they entertained for very long—leaving. Where else would they go? To Alex, it was only prolonging the inevitable. To Cal, their home was there and would never be anywhere else. And to providence, it was a simple fact that their apartment had not flooded and that Cal knew a useful trade and that Alex had fallen a little in love with a dead world long before she resided in one, with her late night trysts with abandoned buildings and decaying lots, and her affinity for plucking lost objects from the gloomy place that they had been left to rot in. Plainly put, this was their home, and they would stand their ground.

Stand their ground they did, as across the city the electricity went out and chaos reigned, violent break-ins rose in the darkness and the two of them took turns guarding the doors and windows, half-asleep, with crowbars across their laps. Only once did anyone breach the threshold, and it was Alex, eyes glaring and teeth flashing, that threatened that faceless man within an inch of his life and terrified him so badly that no one dared to bother them again after that. No one dared bother their neighbors, either, those who had stayed and moved from the flooded floors to the dry ones, taking new vacancies or bunking with one another. In that way, the entire building became something of a safe-haven, albeit one that was not well-stocked.

Slowly, all of the East Coast cities began to resemble Venice, as Venice disappeared beneath the waves like the mystical Atlantis. Some moved further inland and prayed that the rivers would be kind. Some stayed firmly planted in the cities, in upper-level apartments and high-water stilted houses, drifting through the streets in makeshift boats. When the rains poured, the street-rivers swelled and became impassable, but when the skies calmed, a network of waterways emerged from the depths.

Alex was not afraid of the water, and maybe she should have been. Many were, even those that stayed either for lack of a reason or the resources to leave. But Alex, fierce and fearless, when it came to a feat of nature and not a lifetime of working service jobs, would dive in and out of the flooded streets without hesitation, reminded of her inland explorations that now seemed so harmless, eons ago. She was protected, of course, in re-purposed diving gear, the result of a trade of Cal's services.

There was no sewage like the sewage that infiltrated the city street-rivers, not just a conglomeration of everyday litter, but a toxic soup of gasoline, cleaning sprays, and machine oils that coagulated into a suspicious sludge which coated walls and roads and the skin of those brave or foolish enough to travel with bare hands and arms. Worse were the leaking neon signs, the leftover chemicals in the walls that had never been up to code and were being drawn out with the floods. Even so, as time went on, the sweeping water and the raging nature of the storms cleaned much of the streets eventually, though there was the pollution of the dead gas pumps and the radiation from the hospital machines, and so much more to contend with.

Still, Alex, fearless, set out to scavenge that morning as she had so many mornings before, for things to trade with the neighbors or for Cal to use, or for her own use, every now and again. She waded through the waist-deep water, towards the nearest subway station, with a hunch (and her hunches were often legendary, with the faintest hint of prophecy in her) that the pizzeria on the same block would not be picked through yet, and would have some of the soft metal to melt down that Cal had requested.

The pizzeria had been cleared, but whoever had done it had missed a few things that would do Cal well. It was an easy in and out, and though she had hours of daylight ahead of her and a long list of hopeful finds to seek, she could feel herself pulled, as she quite often was, towards the gaping, hungry mouth of the subway station. It was as if the curves of the water cradled her towards the entrance, in a lilting, hunted song that carried with the current, half-imagined and echoing off of the ceramic subway tile buried beneath the water.

Without knowing how she had gotten there, Alex found herself facing the entrance head-on, as the mouth of it stretched down the stairs and into the unseen abyss. It seemed, in that moment, that the only thing she could do was to descend into the depths. After all, who had been down there since it flooded? The allure of the undiscovered, and perhaps also the siren-song, barely there, called to her.

In a tinge of subtle unreality, the fluorescent lights twinkled over-head, like the stars she had not seen in so long, residing in a city that, though half-dead, still gripped tightly to its rampant light pollution. Along the stair bannisters, algae and seaweed twisted upwards, shying from the low haze of the upper sunlight but reaching strange arms to-wards Alex as she descended. Despite the overhead lights, darkness invaded each corner, each small space untouched by the light; shad-ows dodged the faint, remaining glows and crept around the still cars, the high voltage tracks that had been shut off with the trains when it was clear that the rain and flooding had no plans to stop.

It occurred to Alex that she had stupidly forgotten to listen for the electric hum before descending; that she had heard stories from nights gathered with mugs of warm, spiked, something-or-other (slightly re-sembling cider, but it usually wasn't) around the makeshift fire that burned on their balcony, of those unlucky divers who didn't think to check, who ended their lives electrified on live wires.

If she stuck around beyond those stories, until the fire embers were allowed to die and a couple of people still lingered over the ashes, with mugs gone cold and the crisp, cool air of the night closing in around them, she heard other tales—of unknown ocean creatures that swam up from the depths to make new homes in the bellies of the flooded subway tunnels, of the dead-not-dead bodies of those unfor-tunate divers still living-not-living on the platforms, of the mutations that began to befall those unknown creatures of the ocean's depths, now flooded so close to land. Alex could clock Cal's worry across the dead fire, knit brows and frown lines caused not by the fear that the stories would scare her, but that they would inspire her.

And here she was, in the heart of the stories, lured by the ghost of a song and imagined treasures. At the bottom of the sunken staircase stretched a landscape of ceramic tile and algae, long tendrils swaying upright in the water. A train sat still on the tracks, its windows dark. Alex swam towards it, floating over the turnstiles alongside the ticket booths with bars across the front, and past fogged plexiglass layered maps that fostered lake-deep vegetation behind the surface.

The doors to the train were shut, but Alex pried them open easily. There was no reason to head for the train first, in the watery stillness of the former station, except that it stood like a proud, silent ghost on the tracks, and the spirit of curiosity and adventure inside of Alex couldn't help but be pulled toward it, despite it all.

Inside of the car, she could see evidence of life: strange fish darting in and out of the vents and a thick black residue coating the walls; a bed of algae beneath her floating form that carpeted the subway car's tile floor; and, most alarmingly, a spattering of bones in a pile on one of the bench seats.

Undeterred, Alex leaned forward to examine them. They were small and brittle, eaten away to a clean polish by the high levels of acidity in the water. She tucked the bones into her bag for future examination and potential use, and turned her attention to the fish, who glinted a metallic gold and did not stay in view for very long, making her wonder what kind of unseen creatures resided in the vent system along with them. The black residue was equally unsettling—a substance unlike any she had seen before in both color and consistency, appearing dark enough to rival the blackness of the station's unlit corners and burnt-out bulbs, patterned between those still flickering in the ceilings. The metallic fish skirted the walls too, avoiding the black sludge as their tails flashed in the slices of light that bore through the breaks in the fogged window.

The stillness broke, almost imperceptibly at first. The fish, quick and nimble as they were, shuddered out of the car and into the vents with a sense of panic. A rumble sounded a few cars away, followed by a terrible shriek of metal on metal, which carried through the space as though someone were prying open a much more stubborn door than the one Alex had found. The subway car shook subtly, the station lights flickered outside, and then, an unearthly wail echoed through the submerged station, made ghastlier for travelling through the water as it did.

Alex ducked beneath a half-uprooted bench seat and clung to the metal beam as she crouched there, back against the black-sludge-stained wall as the wail curdled the space around her, as all of a sudden, without warning, the doors to the car were forced open and an unfathomable creature pressed through the opening, a wail on her lips and blood on her vicious sharp canines.

She was an amalgamation of the subway's pollution, the radium spills below the surface, the black sludge that coated the walls. Her hair danced in wild, dark clouds above her head, her skin glowed faintly of radiation, aching green, framing a mouthful of sharp, stained teeth set in a thin, high-boned face. Her torso was bare, but wrapped in algae and other types of plant life that thrived out of view of the sun. It curved downward into a tail of sickening black, akin to the sludge, sealed with metallic golden scales and tangled in the floor plants and station cast-offs—plastic wrappers and clothing tags and ticket stubs and shards of broken glass painfully and permanently embedded in her skin. Maybe it was the strangeness of the moment, the eerie wail that had just broken the stillness, but Alex could have sworn that, intermingled with the remnants of humanity's trash, she could see the flash of a familiar apartment key, the petal of a black rose like the kind her downstairs neighbor used to leave on her doorstep after a long day. When she blinked, both had disappeared into the debris cutting into her tail, or had never been there at all.

Her bright eyes, yellow as a burning sun, found Alex crouched beneath the lopsided bench with her dive suit resembling an alien skin stuck fast to her own, eyes wide beneath her helmet as she and the creature, beautiful and terrifying both, locked gazes and studied one another in a curious stand-off. The creature was the first to move, but did not break the gaze; as she moved, the water moved around her as if it were being cut with a knife, split open on her jagged smile.

Face to face with Alex, she grinned a fierce threat, showing off a full mouth of teeth marred by blood and carnage. She did not speak, but a distant wailing tone escaped from the back of her throat, a sound that keened over Alex like a dog whistle: sharp, metallic, too high to be comfortable, a broken note that threatened to break Alex too. She clapped her hands over her ears, and to her surprise, the wailing ceased and the creature's gaze shifted to one of concern. She studied Alex with a new curiosity and then gestured, with one long, clawed finger, for Alex to follow her into the depths of the station.

And maybe it was something in her eyes, an intensity that was both honest and terrifying, but follow her was exactly what Alex did. The odd pair slipped through the wide hallways, now flooded, the peeling and faded advertisements glowering at them from the walls. The schools of strange fish, the tiny mutated water-creatures, gave them a wide berth as they passed, but the creature gliding ahead of Alex didn't spare them a glance as she led them effortlessly deeper into the heart of the station. She led them through twisting tunnels and over rusted turnstiles, over miles of dead tracks to another station on the line, ignoring the deep rumbles from offshoot tracks and darkened tunnels as they swam.

Alex knew the creature ahead of her heard them, at least, because she inclined her head ever-so-slightly towards the noise, and sped up towards their destination just a bit when one sounded. Once, she led them into a dark corner, and Alex watched in horror as something large, scaled, hunting, mouth full of teeth and body vicious and shadowed, slunk past. It was eyeless and swimming blind, but swam as though it could smell them furled away in the corner, and for a moment, Alex forgot to breathe.

When they reached the station—another watery graveyard of stilled train skeletons and odd, glinting fish and dead advertisements—they did not stop but continued up a maintenance hatch, flooded, that landed them on what Alex realized was the empty first floor of the city's once-prestigious art museum. She ascended the hatch, but the creature did not follow, lingering instead in the flooded space with her arms folded over the ledge.

It was here that she first spoke, in a voice raspy and whispered, so unlike the high, clear keen of her wail.

"I dreamed you."

Alex was too taken aback for words and let her blank stare suffice.

"You were like me. There was another with you," the creature continued, undeterred. "I was like you, once."

Wanting more than anything to move this strange conversation off of herself, Alex clamped onto this last admission and forced herself to ask, "What happened?" in a voice far more timid than she would have liked.

The creature acted as if she hadn't spoken, and maybe she hadn't.

"Don't come down here again. Go down this hall; the main stairs are to your right." She moved to disappear back down the hatch, but hesitated, turning back to Alex with her ever-startling stare. Her voice became softer, less direct. "I dreamed you," she whispered again, almost forlorn as she said it. And then, though Alex had felt the tension building and had pushed it to the back of her mind, she leaned in and pressed her lips to Alex's. They were softer and warmer than she had anticipated, gentler than she had assumed, and sent a brilliant shower of fireworks coursing through Alex's head, even as the mermaid placed her clawed hand against Alex's cheek, and then pulled away as easily as she had leaned in.

As if nothing had happened, without even a backwards glance, she turned and swam down the hatch, letting it fall closed with a slam that echoed in the archway of marble and concrete above Alex's head. She found herself standing in the loading dock of the museum—denoted by the peeling signs on the wall—alone and confused, and still with the lingering feeling of the mermaid's lips on hers, haunting her.

She did not tell Cal, for many reasons. She found her way home, bag full of scraps, head muddled as she waded through the middle of the street with the sun setting ahead of her. The sun, which was growing older, in some strange twist of fate. Growing larger, a deeper yellow, sinking like the Earth around it.

It was in this aging glow that she reached their apartment building, climbed the steps until her feet were no longer wading through the pooled water on the first and second floors, and reached their front door. She had to knock; it was bolted thrice and there were no keys. Cal was paranoid, rightfully so, after the chaos of the first few nights without electricity. He answered, and she was suddenly struck with how thin and hollow-boned his face was, how pale he was in the late afternoon glow, but then he shifted and the light cast his shadows differently, and he was just Cal again.

She did not see him much over the next few days, and the silence gave her plenty of time to think about the creature and the flooded subway station, the prophecy of a past dream and the warning of a future trespass, and, admittedly, the intense, yellow-sun stare of the creature from the depths. Life went on, as life does at the end of the world, until Cal emerged from his workshop-cave of a room and she saw just how thin his face had become, how fevered his eyes, how hollow his gaze. He crossed from his bedroom to the kitchen without a word, distracted by his own thoughts, but Alex stopped him halfway.

"Are you sick or something?"

"Huh?" He swung his gaze to her too rapidly for comfort, his eyes tracking across the room in a slightly crazed fashion before landing on her fully.

"You look sick. Just, here—" she reached up to him and pressed the back of her hand flat across his forehead. "No temp. Do you feel—?"

"I'm fine. Really. Just hungry."

She stared after him as he trooped into the kitchen, grabbed a couple of snack bags salvaged from some vacated establishment, and disappeared back in his room with the door firmly shut behind him. She pressed an ear up against the wood, but heard nothing but the occasional rustle, and retreated to her own room to spend another quiet night staring at the ceiling and thinking, with some slight obsession, of the woman in the subway station, no longer a "creature" in her mind's voice, but a beautiful ghost among the fish and seaweed. The dark ceiling danced in her vision, fluorescents peeking at the edge of her filtered perception as she watched her memories cross the space in vivid, hallucinatory detail. Tomorrow. Tomorrow she would go back.

When she dozed off in her half-lucid state, the subway station and the mysterious woman that had emerged from its depths decorated her dreams, too, until she wasn't sure whether she was dreaming or was wide awake again, wading through the flooded hallways with, against all logic, a candle-flame lantern in one hand and a flash of scales in the other that winked at her in the odd light, a sickly green of the same shade she had seen reflected in the shadows on Cal's cheeks. She could feel each footstep, her muscles pushing through the water to mimic her stride on land, her booted feet pressing against the ground as if they were trying to stay rooted there, even as her body pushed her to float again.

Ahead, the darkened tunnel loomed and stretched into a blackness that her feeble light did not reach; the thunderous rumbles sounded in great waves that shook the tracks beneath her feet, and when she looked up, she was face to face with the yellow-sun eyes of the subway, a clawed hand beckoning her foreword, the bruised blue lips forming a summons, before Alex awoke gasping for air in the window light of a full sun, thinking of the burning kiss and the mermaid's hand on her cheek, the haunting familiarity of it all.

She spilled out of bed in a tumble of arms and legs, tossing off the quilt and sliding around the corner in her bare feet to Cal's room. The door was closed and, strangely, locked, though they'd never had any locked doors between one another before. She threw her fists against the door and rocked it on its hinges for how hard she pounded against its feeble frame. It was with this cacophony that she roused Cal and brought him, bleary and blinking slowly, peering into the sunlight from the slight crack between the door and the frame. He was still wearing last night's rumpled clothes, which looked as though they had seen a couple days' wears, and when he looked at Alex, recognition was slow to cross his face. He looked dazed, uncomprehending in Alex's wake, and even more sickly than he had last night.

She met his fogged gaze for a moment and then, wordless, pushed gently past him into the room. His curtains were drawn, black-out curtains that cast the room in a devastating shadow, and every surface including the floor was strewn with books, thrown open to middle pages. There were notebook scribbles, and scribbles that trailed across the furniture in Cal's messy handwriting, none of it easily decipherable. Her eyes swept around the room, not clinging to any one thing in the chaos.

"Cal?"

"I think I'm dying," he murmured. "I had to be sure."

Her throat clenched, her voice a bare gasp in her jumbled mouth as she forced out the words. "Why would you think that?"

"It's radiation. I had to be sure," he repeated.

Anger washed over her like a red-hot wave, drowning her like the flooded subway tunnel. He had stayed inside. He had been protected. She had taken on the burden of the danger of scavenging, and she had taken that burden gladly, so that she might protect her older brother, her last companion at the end of this world, as he had once protected her. And yet. And yet. If he said it was radiation, it was. He was a genius, unfailingly and unflinchingly so, and even dazed and unfocused he would know. Which could only mean that she had brought something contaminated into the apartment, something that had spent a considerable amount of time in his close proximity. She had done this to him, and she couldn't even pinpoint a time, a place, an offending object. The pain of it nearly overtook her, a grief that threatened to shut down her synapses and collapse her entirely.

The single rational thought that pressed through the wave of rage and grief was of the strange woman in the subway tunnel, with her intense gaze and her sure movements and the way she had beckoned Alex forward in the dream-not-dream. There were answers below. This was an undisputed fact that, once considered, could not be ignored. This was the fact that drew her running ragged around the apartment, seeking her boots and dive suit and a spare for Cal, poking and prodding him into it as he moved numbly, trying, stumbling, being righted by Alex who had never felt so strong or so heinous in that moment.

She half-carried him, running down the street, the strange duo silhouetted by a fresh and early sun rising on a broken city, down the steps and into the depths of the dark underground, Alex searching frantically for the strange woman, as she moved through the station with Cal supported on her arm. The metallic fish flashed and scattered as she rushed over the turnstiles and past the advertisements and towards the subway car where she had first seen the woman. When she pried the doors open and found it empty of everything but the questionable black sludge climbing the walls and choking the vents, she let out a howl that, even under the water, echoed down the tunnels for miles—a cry and a call all at once.

The call was answered, first by a disturbance in the subtle movement of the water and then by a shrill cry that matched her own and scared away the fish and floating creatures that haunted the station.

The woman appeared, following her earsplitting wail with her strange tail gleaming in the remaining lights as it flicked around with a mind of its own. "Help him. Help him, please." She did not know if she could be heard under the water, but she hoped the expression painted across her face would suffice. She did not know if the strange woman could hear her, if she could help her, but she did know that Cal wouldn't survive to the end of the miles of track that led to the maintenance hatch she had clambered out of not so long ago.

The woman said nothing, did not wail again, but extended one slender hand towards Cal and pulled him with her into the depths, away from Alex, who tried wildly to follow and could not keep up with the woman. She saw the last wisp of that serpentine tail disappear into the darkness as she fell behind, and then let herself drop to the ground, trust again misplaced and Cal out of her reach and beyond her saving. She willed herself to run out of air there on the abandoned, flooded tracks, to rot in the belly of the overflowed ocean for some other unlucky scavenger to find, to let her corpse serve as a warning to any that travelled so far.

And then, like an omen, the woman reappeared with Cal, who was not Cal, who was truly Cal, at her side. His skin carried her sheen, his face thin-boned but no longer so hollow as it had been, his torso ending in a curling, sinuous tail that wavered in the water beneath him, rife with the sickly green glow of radiation, painfully pressed shards of shattered iron, and the black sludge that had coated the subway walls—the same black sludge Alex realized must coat some strange salvaged piece of metal that now resided in Cal's landbound room. His eyes met hers, unclouded.

She looked, then, to the woman, floating in front of her with a gaze that meant many things, *he is safe* among them, but more prominent, a siren's song, a beckoning that Alex recognized from the ghost of a dream and the ghost of a memory both, a clawed hand extended and a promise, unspoken, for the creatures that newly resided in the darkness, never again to be separated through ages and ages onward.

MONICA ROBINSON (mrobinsonwrites.com) is a queer experimental poet and recycled artist, mixing mediums to create fresh works of exploratory literature. She is eternally haunted by the rural Midwestern landscape in which she grew up, and she has been writing her brand of the weird and the wild ever since.

Monica is the author of Exit Wounds, EARTH IS FULL; GO BACK HOME, bury me in iron and ivy: a midwestern gothic, relayed in pieces, *and is currently working on her first full-length fiction work. She has also been published in* Persephone's Daughters, Mookychick Mag, *and* Stone of Madness Press, *and currently works with* Sword & Kettle Press *and* Frayed Edge Press *on social media management and content creation.*

SWEET WATER

Jess Koch

Before I was born, I dreamt of the sea. It's the only thing I remember from whatever comes before this. Memories of another life, perhaps. Or memories from my mother, transferred in her womb. The smell is what I remember most clearly. And that sting of salt on my tongue. Then the spray of sea in the wind. The violent rage of waves in a storm.

Before I ever knew anything about Ankou, the river, or Inés, I knew the sea.

The river had been dormant for more than a hundred years when I was born. Its waters were clear and sweet but no longer able to heal the sick. My village prayed to Ankou, the collector of the dead, to send his sister to earth once more, to reunite with the river. And Ankou answered their prayers with me: a baby girl born on a dark winter solstice night. The first in generations.

After I bled for the first time, my father and the other village men took me to the river. I was just barely twelve. The rest of the village—

women, children, my mother—came to the banks of the river and watched my father lead me into the water.

My white silk dress bloomed like a lily in the current. My father dipped two of his fingers in the river and drew a wet line down my forehead, over the bridge of my nose and my lips. He said I should not be afraid, that this was the greatest honor I could offer my family, the very reason I was born. I was a goddess, he said. And a goddess should never be afraid.

But I was afraid. I cried out and he said, "Hush now, Aliénor." And he lay me down in the water, pressing my shivering body under the surface. He pushed me lower and deeper until my back struck against the stony riverbed. I held my breath, I tried to stay still, but I needed air. I thrashed and clawed at my father's strong arms, scratched through his skin. His blood swirled away on the current. But still he held me down.

And when I couldn't hold my breath any longer, when my lungs burned, and my eyes went black, a rush of water filled my insides.

The river swallowed me whole.

My mother visited me often at first. She sat on the shore and sang the songs her own mother used to sing. They were in an old tongue, the language of my mother's family, the only language she spoke. But I never learned to understand it. I never learned to understand *her*. The only words of her song that I recognized were in the last lines, before it looped back to its beginning: à la mer. To the sea.

After a time, her belly began to swell.

And one day, she brought a small bundle to the river and cried as she unwrapped the blankets, lowered a naked infant into the river. His pale body looked like it was floating on the surface in her hands. He was impossibly small. Impossibly still.

My mother wept. Her tears fell over the child and into the water. I tasted the salt in her sorrow. I washed water over the boy, but there was nothing I could do. The river could not heal him. I could not heal him. He was already with Ankou, shepherded from the earth.

I wanted to tell her I was sorry, but even if I could speak, she wouldn't understand my words, wouldn't understand how much I meant them.

She left with the boy held close to her chest, humming her song while she cried.

It was the last time I ever saw her.

Years passed and many others came to be healed. Some came to mend cracked bones and cut skin. Others came to heal their failing hearts or broken minds. Some were so sick they crawled with the last of their strength just to reach the edge of the water.

Many left healed. But others were too sick and they died on my shores. I carried their bodies on the current all the way to where the river met the sea.

I felt myself waning. It seemed that every time I healed, my human self slipped away a little more down river. I knew that one day, there would be nothing left of her. And I would only be the goddess.

On the warmest day of one summer, a woman came to the river. Her name was Inés and she was dying. Her skin had a sick pallor, her dark hair was falling out, and when she coughed, blood came up from her lungs.

Still, she was more beautiful than anyone I had ever seen.

She lay down in the shallows at the edge of the river and prayed for my help. For three days I pushed and pulled the healing water over her body.

On the first day, she slept in silence, waking only to cough and spit up blood, which I swept away. She was a delicate, lovely thing. I watched her chest rise and fall and counted every breath. The slow ones, the ones with too much time in between them, the ones that caught in her throat. The count didn't matter, it only mattered that there was another breath after the last.

On the second day, her eyes opened. They were a deep green like the moss in the riverbed. Her skin was flushed with fever.

On the third day she sat up and drank from the river with shaking hands. The sweet water dripped down her chin, her neck, her chest. Then she lay back down on the grass, her legs still submerged in the river, her loose dress drifting and swaying under the surface. Her gaze shifted past the river, past the trees, to some place beyond, as though she could see something that wasn't there. Sometimes, the dying would say they could see Ankou on the other side of the river. Skeletal hands outstretched. Waiting for them.

I became fixated on her fingers. Long and dark and intertwined with the grass. I imagined those fingers touching my skin. Sweeping through my hair like it was river grass. Climbing down my neck.

Her eyes slowly closed, and as I watched her sleep, I noticed the way her dress clung to her breasts, the way her lips parted with shallow breaths, the way her shoulders glistened with wetness and sunlight.

And in that moment, I did something I'd never done before. Something I thought I would never do. I gathered myself in the reeds and pulled up the roots that became legs once more, and stood. I was naked, hair dripping wet, the current rushing past my thighs. But the river did not surrender all of me. My left arm was still a flowing mass of algae caught on a submerged branch. My right eye was a stone in the silt at my feet.

Inés woke as I lowered myself into the shallows beside her, placing my head on the grass near her hand. Her deep green eyes narrowed as she reached out toward my face. Warm fingertips brushed my cheek.

"Are you the goddess of this river?" she asked.

"Yes, I'm Aliénor." Though even as I said it, the words were wrong on my clumsy human tongue. My name *was* Aliénor but what claim did I hold on that life? That girl was lost to the river so long ago. Carried away to the sea. I was the unnamed goddess now. Kin of Ankou.

"You're so beautiful," she said, as her eyes drifted closed again.

I sang my mother's song to Inés, passing over the words phonetically, still not knowing what they really meant. My voice sounded both familiar and strange at once, and I realized that I was hearing my mother's voice. And for the first time in a long time, I mourned for her.

"You know, my mother used to sing me that song," Inés said, when she woke that night. "*Oh brittle bones, return to the sea, before the tide comes in and takes you from me,*" she sang, translating the words, her voice lilting over the notes.

"Your mother was from the coast?"

Inés nodded. "I was too. But our people are gone now. I always meant to go back but … " the dim moonlight illuminated the curves of her face. The reflection of the river danced across her skin. "Do you do this with all of the people that you heal?"

"No," I said. "This is the first time."

"Why now? Why me?"

She pressed closer to me. I felt her breath against my lips. I felt the warmth emanating from her body on my bare skin.

"Do you miss it?" she asked. Not waiting for my answer, she reach out and her fingers drew a line up my arm and across my collarbone.

"Miss what?"

"Being like this. Human."

I pressed my palm against her side, feeling the stability of bone under her skin, like she was made of earth and not water.

"I'm not sure." The truth of those words surprised me as I said them.

"Why don't you leave?"

"I am part of the river; this is what I was born to do."

"No one is born to do anything," Inés said. "Besides, I don't see a river. I see a woman. She brushed hair away from my empty eye socket. "One who has given a lot of herself already."

"I can't," I said, because I didn't know what else to say.

"Aren't you lonely here?" she asked.

"There are always people coming to the river."

"Not that kind of lonely," Inés said. She tilted my face toward hers and kissed my cheek. Her lips found mine and her tongue slipped into my mouth. Her feverish warmth spread through me. I wanted to stay in her warmth forever.

We woke holding each other in the shallows as a mist rose from the river, and the sun burned the low sky with an orange haze. Her fever had worsened overnight. Droplets of sweat clung to her forehead like dew. I kissed her cheek. Her sweat tasted like my mother's tears, like the sea in my dreams.

It was time for me to return to the river, so she could be properly healed. But as I tried to slip away, she reached out for my hand and pulled me back to her.

"Don't go," she said. Her eyes were closed, her words quiet.

"I have to heal you."

She laced her fingers in mine and opened her eyes halfway. Just enough that I could see the rising sun reflected in a glint of green in her irises. "I cannot be healed, Aliénor."

"Why not?"

"There's a persistent rot in my bones. Even if you heal me, it would only return when I leave the river."

"Then stay with me."

She drew me in close, kissed me with cracked lips. "I wish I could." Her breath tasted sweet with sickness.

"I will keep you safe."

Inés pulled away and sat up. Her expression changed to something strange, something I'd never seen in her face before. Anger. Her dark brows pulled together and she shook her head.

"For how long? Until your hair grows into river grass? Until your bones have petrified to stone? Until your blood is nothing but water for others to drink?"

"What do you mean?"

"When I came here, I thought I would just stay forever. But that isn't how this works, is it?"

I put my only hand over my missing eye and circled the hollowness with my fingertips.

"It's a sacrifice," she continued. "Your body in exchange for healing the sick."

I wanted to tell her she was wrong. I wanted to *prove* to her that I was a goddess. But when I looked down at my reflection in the rippling water, I did not see a divine being. I did not see the image of Ankou's sister with golden eyes and skin glowing like the moon. Instead, I saw a woman. Brown hair tangled with algae and one blue eye staring back at her. Blue like her mother's eyes.

Inés died in my arms that day, and I carried her body to the coast. Not on the current, but on the sturdy bones of my back. On the earth. I followed the river all the way to the end, where the waves cascaded up the shoreline and swept over my feet, the air tasted of salt and brine, and the ocean stretched out endlessly on the horizon and disappeared into the sky.

"I brought us home, Inés. To the sea."

JESS KOCH is a fiction writer, software engineer, and graduate of the Stonecoast MFA program. She writes strange stories from a pre-civil war colonial somewhere in New England with her partner, dog, and probably a few ghosts. She can be found at jesskoch.com and on Twitter and Instagram @byjesskoch.

RESISTANCE

Morgan Melhuish

I∝V

It appears on the walls of Louvain overnight. Just walking to work I've seen it three, four times … daubed in whitewash along an alley-way; scratched into a door and the metal of a lamp post; on the shutters of a shop.

I have to ask Sister Agatha what it means.

"It's Ohm's law. You use it to work out the relationship between voltage, current and resistance." I knew she'd know. There's a reason she's nicknamed the Divine Spark, a Godsend when the generator plays up in the convent. Mother Superior doesn't like us to remember, but we all had lives before we were nuns.

Intellectual graffiti. That's typical for a university city.

As the Germans advance across Belgium I know Ohm's Law isn't just an electrical equation. Whoever has plastered this on the streets, it is a message to the people of Louvain.

Resistance.

These past weeks, we've tracked their progress, listening to reports on the wireless, then compline, as if a show of faith could keep them back, like a vampire and a crucifix; as if a few prayers would make us sleep more soundly.

When the Germans began their invasion of the country, the Mother Superior held a meeting. What should we do? Dozens of conflicting voices, honking and cackling like unsettled geese; it was a waste of my time. I just held my breath in dread anticipation—along with the rest of Belgium. I felt it was a certainty they'd come.

Some of our sisters have fled towards France, to bigger convents, or the coast. I've never been one to run. It just delays the inevitable.

I hold the door of the library open for Sister Agatha. We take handfuls of our habits to allow us to climb the swirling marble of the staircase quickly, two steps at a time. Above us, a universe of stars meet in an ornate chandelier, such is the splendour of the library.

"Do you think they will?" I ask her.

"Not if they've any sense," she replies.

I already know my relationship to resistance and running. At a very young age I learnt the consequences. I dismiss such troubling thoughts; my father calling me a demon child ...

"Still," Sister Agatha adds with a smile, "men are not known for their good sense, are they?"

I take her hand and give it a squeeze as we slip along the corridor to the archives.

Piece by piece we have helped Mr Delannoy catalogue the works the library holds. He assures us that other libraries already do this; that they know which books, manuscripts and incunabula they hold. All I know is that libraries have always been my sanctuary. Even before the convent, I would hide from having to go home from school with tales of water sprites, Chicken Licken, goblins and storks. The Catholic university library is no different—it's a safe space I've come to treasure.

"Morning," I tell the statue in the centre of the room.

Sister Agatha, practical as ever, winds the mechanism that will crack open all the windows and disperse the musty smell of dusty tomes, and bring a cool breeze to the space.

She laughs. "One day he'll respond, and then what will you do?"

"We'll go for tea and chocolate cake. He's paying." I nod towards the golden figure, and Agatha's smile lights up the glass-domed room more than the bright August morning.

When the library was built, no expense was spared. It is a repository of baroque opulence as well as a stronghold for theological doctrine and intellectual rigour. Even now, along with the written acquisitions, other artefacts are donated in wills and beneficiaries to the university and the church. I don't know how long the statue has been here, but he looks at home amongst the dark varnished bookshelves and thick burgundy carpet. *The Midas Boy* is handsome from his golden grin all the way down to his gold leaf buckles. He is raised high on a six-foot fat plinth while a golden chandelier drops down towards his crown.

Then there are two oddities no one can explain. First, a wrought iron fence, like stubby park railings, encircles the plinth; secondly dull-grey manacles secure his ankles. Mr Delannoy hadn't a clue and stared at me as if I were simple when I raised it.

"You've forgotten the superstitions of the low countries," Agatha said. "Don't you remember? Iron contains restless souls, dulls magic and repels evil."

"This is a university, a religious one at that."

She raised her hands in supplication and then brought them together in prayer, winking at me. "Just a suggestion."

I can only feel pity for my shackled statue.

Later I'm stood on a ladder, retrieving an armful of books, when I see them. I cry out and, for a moment, I believe I'll lose my balance. The volumes fall in a shower of spines, hitting the plush carpet with a dull thud as I grasp for the wooden rails.

"What is it? Not more spiders," Sister Agatha teases.

"Get up here, now."

From our vantage point we can see German soldiers marching along the streets. It was only a matter of time, but the reality of it shocks me.

"Oh my goodness." Agatha kisses her crucifix.

Bringing order to the chaos in here seems suddenly pointless, now the world is upside down.

We watch the soldiers, grey-green uniforms and helmets, a faceless mass from this distance. It's like when we watch summer storms, holding out for the lightning, the sheer force of raindrops thrumming into flash floods. This a deluge of death.

Sister Agatha's body is so close to mine I imagine I can feel her quickened heartbeat. A frisson of expectation. Why must I think of her as Louvain falls? Everything is in tumult now, free falling like the titles I dropped … My soul is an open book just willing her to read me. She steadies herself with a hand on my shoulder. I feel the pressure, the warmth.

A temptation I'd gladly succumb to.

When I took my vows I was grateful no other would touch me again. I was entering a world an arm's length from reality—a place of repentance—and I had a lot to regret.

I killed my mother as she gave birth to me.

The child that grew still born within me …

The little deaths my father inflicted.

I was glad when he sent me away.

Prayer will not save my soul, but it has brought reflection. I wonder, had my mother lived, if she would have stopped him? Would she have had the strength?

If I was his demon child, what sort of monster was he?

Mother Superior says we should forgive. I've not the grace for that. Not yet.

Prayer and time has brought some sense of solace. Now it is I who want to touch.

I reach for Sister Agatha's hand on my shoulder, take it in mine.

"Hail Mary, blessed are thee amongst women. Be our defence against the wickedness of men. Bless Sister Agatha, keep her and save her. I commend her to your care. Amen."

"Amen," she whispers.

We have stopped looking at the soldiers. Our gaze is filled with each other.

Three days into the German occupation of Louvain, and the air vibrates with tension. There is only expectation. We pray, eat, go to the library ... we watch from the window. These soldiers, they're the puppets of the Kaiser, good boys, doing as they're told. I've seen lads like that walking to the seminary, all angelic, but on their way back they're scrapping in the street. We walk a knife edge. These soldiers are not much older than schoolboys themselves. Not much older than me.

"Back again?" Mr Delannoy asks.

"They're not going to catalogue themselves," Agatha tells him.

None of us need to say we feel safer amongst old papers and manuscripts than anywhere else in the city.

"Idle hands, I suppose," he says, stoically. "Time to see my favourite piece of the collection?"

We have all the time, and none of it. In the library, in Louvain, life is in limbo.

Mr Delannoy leads us to one of the building's many anterooms.

"This is it." In the glass case a large lump of something rests. It looks ancient.

"Is it stone?"

"Wood."

The surface is covered with dozens of carvings: devilish forms with horns and forked tail, squid, flowers, something that could be a Norse rune. Mr Delannoy fumbles with a set of keys and opens the display case.

"Here." He passes it to us. It is heavier than I expected. I run my fingers into the twisting shapes I can't identify, reminded of the examples of Georgian script I've seen at the library, the Mkhedruli alphabet.

"Where's it from?" I ask.

"Easter island." We all know of the Pacific island named after the day it was discovered, like some sort of miracle. Only, it had always been there. The people who lived there knew of its existence. They were building statues, carving letters, long before we arrived on the scene.

"It's a language, isn't it?"

"Of sorts. Academics call the text Rongorongo. It's incredibly rare, incredibly precious. People from all over the world have come to look at it, to take pictures and rubbings of the glyphs."

We pass it back, suddenly nervous of its importance.

"They want to understand it." I tell him.

"Of course."

I think of the Bible, how we are supposed to believe in every word but also to see it as a parable, as a series of teachings … and yet we are not supposed to interrogate the text. I overheard that phrase being used by some students. We are not supposed to question.

"And has it been translated?" Sister Agatha asks.

"Not yet."

The carvings have not yielded their secrets. They resist. Mr Delannoy locks the cabinet up again.

"What I love, especially now ... in uncertain times ... is communication. The desire to speak, to say something to others, to the future. This could be a shopping list or a poem, a religious text or a warning. What matters is that it is here, it represents a cultured civilisation. Whatever happens in the future, our writings, our communications must survive."

It has been six days now. In the city there are dangerous men everywhere. I feel their eyes on us as we walk the streets. Their attention and August's heat, the proximity of Sister Agatha, the itch of my habit, it all conspires to make me sweat and burn with shame.

Yesterday, in the convent, we celebrated the feast day of the apostle Bartholomew. There were special prayers for the martyr, killed for converting the Armenian King to Christianity, his skin flayed from his body. The image the Mother Superior conjured for us made me nauseous. What will the punishment be for my conversion?

I trip on an uneven paving stone, my shoe catches, and I'm falling forwards. Instantly Agatha is steadying me; her arm holds me.

"Lift your eyes to the glory of the Lord, sister," she says, but I'm too concerned with this mortal realm.

Especially now.

Why did everything have to come together like this? Love and war.

"Good morning." In the archive, the manacled boy smiles beatifically down at me, golden as a halo. I wonder how long he will last now the Germans are looting. Agatha winds the winch for the windows, and the day should start like clockwork, as if she has wound it up and let go.

Instead, she almost crumples as she sits down heavily. "What's the use? We're just waiting for death."

I want to tell her not to be silly, while there's life, there's hope. That I need her . . . God forgive me, I'm being selfish. She's only voicing thoughts I've had for days.

I kneel in front of her, take her hands in mine and she pours out her soul.

"When they sent me to the convent, that was it. No more mother or father, no more brother and sister, only Christ and the nuns. They told me maybe I'd get better, if my belief was strong enough, and off they went, a problem solved. I couldn't see how, sending me to the only place women are everywhere. I couldn't see how when I knew I wasn't ill. I wasn't unnatural. I've spent so long denying myself, denying a part of me, it was almost like it no longer existed. That it didn't matter. And now with the Germans ... everything's a mess. And I do exist and I do matter. What a time to learn it."

"I know, I know." I try to soothe her. Sister Agatha's skin is milky white. We intertwine fingers, then palm to palm. I kiss her hand.

The library is our sanctuary.

Underneath the statue, everything is golden, and I gasp in sun beams.

*

It is late afternoon, and I'm watching dust motes dance in shafts of light. Harsh German voices drift through the windows, and I cringe. How can I be so blissful when everything else is going to Hell?

Then there is gunfire. The shots are distant but the sound is unmistakable. Everything freezes at that moment … we hold our breath, the very building seems to tense, and even the dust stops moving. There are more shots—retaliation, I suppose. A rapid ricochet, brutal in its sudden burst.

The city's weapons were taken away at the start of the month, with warnings that only the Belgian army was allowed to take any action against the Hun. Does that mean more soldiers are here? I draw Agatha close.

"What should we do?" she asks. "If we leave now … "

It's impossible to know. We might get caught in the crossfire now or later.

We don't move.

The gunfire dies down.

"There's one thing I'd like to do, before we go. Though you'll think me mad."

Dragging a chair across the room, I stand on it and reach through the railings around the plinth.

"You're letting him go?"

"It doesn't seem fair. He can't run from the Germans."

Every day he's been with us, our constant companion. *The Midas Boy* … a gift that's a curse.

We all have these gifts.

In the story, the child is doomed by his father. His wish for gold becomes his undoing. Just like our Lord in Gethsemane. He must have felt all His powers and foreknowledge a curse, knowing what was to come, knowing what had to happen.

When I look at the burnished boy, I feel the same as when I look at our Lord's pitiful body, wounds and all, hanging from the cross. His gift is survival, against the odds, because of them perhaps. Just as our Lord returned, so this statue will endure.

Agatha's gift is love, a strength she's tried to hide.

And mine … ?

The manacles are old. When I shake them there's a rattle from within. "I wish we had Delannoy's bunch of keys."

"You are crazy," she laughs.

"They'll melt him down for medals."

Then I've pulled the manacles apart. Was it their age? Or were they just for show? Part of the artwork all along? It's done now, and he is released.

We hurry through the city streets. The soldiers want to teach us a lesson. They know examples must be made, strength must be shown, the enemy must be subjugated. The men make house calls, rounding up the occupants and shooting them. I am simultaneously transfixed and repelled by bodies struggling, a runaway shot in the back, screams, silences and prayers …

August is the month we celebrate the Assumption of Mary. By the time we reach the convent, I've already seen too many women go where I will not follow. Agatha whispers prayers under her breath; my fingers rub around my rosary. Even though I want to, there are just too many of them. I'll never remember all of their faces.

We are late for vespers, but join the others, quickly slipping into their ranks in the chapel. Mother Superior has noticed, of course, but instead of a harsh glare and reprimands, her face is full of relief and gratitude. After the concluding prayer and verse, as the others file out to supper, she calls to us.

"Thanks be to God for your safe return. There's been nothing but gunfire all evening. How were the streets?"

How to tell this elderly woman all we have seen? To shatter her faith in humanity.

"Bad," Agatha says, as if she is describing trying to navigate the crush of students on graduation day.

Our Mother Superior places a hand on my shoulder. Her bony hands squeeze my flesh in the closest she comes to emotion.

"God forgive them. Now, let's feed the body as we've fed the soul. We must be prepared for whatever the night brings."

We bob our thanks and join the others. Over the meal, we are back to panic and flapping, the honking geese of the farmyard. I thought I'd given that up when I came here. There are more questions we don't want to answer, about what's happening outside. Speculation is rife, and I prickle all over with terror, knowing what I've seen.

Even stacking dishes, someone says, "They're just as Christian as us, they'd never come here." Fate has been tempted, nausea rises within me. I'm grateful when compline begins.

Of course it's during prayers that they come. Five soldiers step into the chapel, and we watch them, our voices wavering for a moment before Mother Superior continues with the canticle of Simeon, "my eyes have seen thy salvation," and we follow her example, speaking as one.

This only serves to wrong foot them. The energy they arrived with dissipates, and for a moment I feel we're fending them off with faith.

Mother Superior leads us in prayer. Her voice is steady; the waves and rhythm of the words are a comfort I hadn't expected. Until one pushes over a candlestick, the flame gutters in a splash of wax on the stone floor. It is the sound that makes us shudder, the reverberating clang. Then another push.

You have to admire her. Even now she is forgiving them their trespasses.

These men are unbound—lawless and wild. Their leader raises his gun and fires. An explosion of masonry. I'm ashamed that I cry out with the other women.

"Noctem quietam et finem perfectum concedat …" Mother Superior never reaches the end of the blessing. Instead, she falls backwards, the force of the bullet searing through her. She is mercifully dead within moments.

I cross myself and commend her to God's keeping. My hope for a place in Heaven has never been more than a wistful daydream. I wish I had her fervour, her belief. I hope she's found His eternal grace.

Compline curtailed, there is finally silence.

"Outside," the leader barks, gesturing with the gun. "Now."

The summer skies are choked with smoke, an artificial night of the Germans' making. They've set the city ablaze. I see them, so thrilled, so chuffed with what they've done. Their pride dances with the flames reflected in their eyes.

"You are spies," the soldier tells us. "You are men in hiding."

I can tell where this is headed even as my sisters protest. I'm not surprised when they demand we strip. I capitulate quite easily. It's when my chemise is halfway over my head that I hear the shot. The air is still warm on my nakedness as I look to the others hurrying to obey, and Sister Catherine who did not. So many layers to remove, to hide who I was.

At my side, Sister Agatha is like a newborn, and I try not to think about how we lay together mere hours ago. She is everything to me, and now we are chattel in their eyes. They look us over, conferring.

"You, you, you." They want us for now. Six of us.

"We will have a party, yes?" The question is purely rhetorical as, still naked, one soldier marches us back inside. As we walk, I flinch at the sound of gunfire. I don't need to look back to know what has happened to my sisters. I can feel myself retreating, going to the places my father sent me. Where are our angels when we need them? The statues of the convent, their faces are as impassive as always.

"Keep walking." I reach for Agatha's hand. I hear her sobs but I can't look at her. "Don't give them any reason ... please."

I half-drag her inside.

When the men join us, there is no trace of what they've just done. There is a hunger in their eyes, a limitlessness that makes me shiver with remembrance. Nothing is beyond these men. Not even laying with the brides of Christ.

"You two, kiss." The commander laughs.

I hadn't let her go.

"No," Agatha whimpers. I turn to her tear stained face.

"I'm sorry," I tell her.

"No," she keeps repeating, and I reach out to her, closing my eyes.

"Kiss!" The soldiers are insistent. I hear the click of a pistol.

"I don't want to die. I don't want you to die." I lean in.

We kiss. A parody of passion. Both of us crying now. Why do men spoil everything good and holy?

I only open my eyes when we are pulled apart. Their leader has Agatha, and he is dragging her to a cell. One of the others has my wrist in a tight grip. It's been so long since I was held like this. I don't offer any resistance ... I∝V ... I think of the graffiti, I think of Agatha explaining it to me. I think of the vows I made: poverty, chastity, and obedience.

"This way, sir," I tell the soldier.

As he forces his tongue into my mouth, little does he know the demon within. I may be withdrawing, into the past, into myself, as his hands wander. I feel myself surrender and resist all at the same time.

Let him do as he wants. His squeeze stirs up embers I hoped long extinguished. Unknown, they've been smouldering away, scarring my soul.

His touch is too much.

I meekly go to my single bed with its stiff starched sheets. In another life we might have been sweethearts. He looks like a lad I used to know growing up, tanned from working outdoors. I used to be his colour; now I'm virginal again. He starts to remove his shirt.

A wall and a world away I can hear Agatha and her terrible cries. The sound rents my soul.

"Let me," I tell him, my mind racing.

I'm by his side in a quick movement. I stroke his bare chest with one hand, the other is at his buckle. I can feel his hardness pushing at the material of his trousers. He moans and then chuckles. I loosen his belt, pull it clean of the loops, and unzip his fly. I distract him with a kiss and let him awkwardly struggle to get clean of his keks. He hops, a leg caught … it would be comical if this boy wasn't here to rape me. I use his imbalance to my advantage, and he falls, smacking his head on the corner of the bed. His belt is already a noose as I start to strangle him. I pray for the strength as he fights against me. He slips to the flagstone floor, and I stand on his back and pull. He is spent and so am I. On the farm, father would make me snap the necks of the chickens. It was never as exhausting as this.

Agatha screams, and I've the soldier's gun in my trembling hands.

I was damned from the moment I entered the world. I might as well be my own avenging angel; be hers. God forgive me, but it's easier with the pistol and at such short range …

The noise must alert the others, but they're momentarily occupied. They can't imagine women resisting.

It's what we've spent our lives doing. Just existing—living in their world.

Poor Agatha. She cries hysterically, and I'm thinking, just thinking. Should I kill the other three? Should I try? Should I run? I can't have long. If I leave the other nuns they're as good as dead. But what use will the time I buy them be? There's no escape, no happy ending for any of us.

Agatha whimpers as I search for the commander's gun. I've two now.

"Bless you," she says as I leave the cell. I squeeze my eyes shut, tight against the tears.

Every face inside is a ghost from my youth. They remind me of the child I once was. There are parts of myself I like to think I can shut off, hide away … It's just not true. I can't deal with them. Even Agatha—especially her. I should go and say something to her … tell her… but what's the use? There are no words. Nothing I can say will change what's happened to her.

I suddenly realise I don't even know her name. Not her real name, the one from before she was a nun, before her vows. Back when she was a woman.

Instead, I stand on the threshold in fresh robes, trying not to look at the crumpled forms by the wall and the women they once were.

It's not just the killing that's senseless. It's these troops. They tell themselves that what they're doing is correct, they're just following orders. These men kid themselves their autonomy is not their own. There is only black and white for them. The soldiers don't see the kaleidoscope colours of fire as they raze another home, they're blind as justice to the crimson of blood. Worse than that, some have lost their humanity entirely.

Smoke still chokes the air, but in the embers of the skyline I see that beyond the convent all is in ruins. The very fabric of the city is flame, or has been. The criminal courts have been gutted. It's as if the Germans believe they can erase law and order from Louvain with the destruction of a building. They should be ashamed. If they followed the law they wouldn't be here. Instead, they've ignored charters "scribbled on scraps of paper." They've tossed them away and brought chaos and killing instead. So many homes and businesses burning, all the lives they represent …

I feel the loaded pistol beneath my habit.

What now? Am I to become like those soldiers? Haven't I already? An Old Testament God taking eyes and teeth. I must resist the rage within, the hurt and fear.

I shudder. Underfoot, the damp of dew grounds me, the cool of the night air brings back my reason. There will be others out there who are in need. There are souls who might need saving. Miracles are beyond me, but there must be someone I can help.

*

I slip through the streets. Splinters of glass lie like confetti after a wedding, the remains of bodies, sticky pools of blood like tar. I keep to the shadows, carefully picking my way around the obstacles. Those I meet, all in need of shelter, I send to the convent.

The library is a husk. Its entrance a dark hollow mouth like the scream I can feel building within me. I grab for the wall, but it offers no support. I'm falling to my knees, the opposite of prayer. Pure despair at this violation of knowledge.

There's the sound of boots. I quickly stand and press myself against the wall. On the street, soldiers have come, turning my way. It's ridiculous to think I can imagine myself invisible, a childish hope that if I close my eyes they won't see me. They're just silhouettes for now, three shadows gaining form and mass, coming into focus.

There's no choice but the library – it was inevitable I'd return

I lift my robes and dash inside the smoking building, knowing the movement will catch their attention but hoping I'll be too swift for shots. I run into a barrier of heat and push into its resistance. Relief is quickly replaced with the realisation I'm in the abyss. Devastation is everywhere. Smoke stings my eyes, and I am blind. Burning fills my throat. The stench of petrol threatens to overwhelm me. This is a glimpse into Hell.

The scripts in Hebrew, Chaldaic, Mr Delannoy's treasured Easter Island carvings, the Latin incunabula … the messages of our ancestors—all gone. All that knowledge, those thoughts and facts, the words and phrases, the poetry and praise … charred, unreadable pages now. The library is a ruin of enlightenment, and I cannot escape its confines.

There are no words.

I drop to my knees. The smoke is thinner here, and I bring the thick sleeve of my robe across my face with a pressed arm. There are no flames—here at least the fire has run its course. Its damage is everywhere, though, and it is eerily quiet aside from the occasional creaking and groaning as if the building is gasping in pain, gulping the last of the night's air.

Will the soldiers follow? I crawl across the atrium as fast as I can, eyes watering, coughs racking my body, heading towards the stairs. There are voices outside now. I catch hold of the banister to pull myself up, but recoil at its searing heat. I switch arms and with my unscarred hand I gain purchase on the marble stairs. Upright, I scrabble for the steps.

I can hear the soldier's reaction to crossing the threshold, and I can dimly make them out across the foyer, which means they can see me. I think of Agatha, the days we spent here, scurrying up these steps. I move.

2, 4, 6, 8…

My way is blocked and, lifting my head, I don't believe what's in front of me.

A shot rings out and ricochets off the banister, so close I scream with my singed throat. It's a terrible sound.

Immediately, my one good hand is up in half-surrender, the other still covers my nose and mouth. Behind me, impossibly, *The Midas*

Boy stands, as if he's descended and is waiting to be announced at a ball. How did he get here?

The Germans are coming towards us. Shouting through the smoke. Guns waving. A grinding squeal comes from the library and, in their brief distraction, I slip behind the statue.

"I'm sorry," I whisper as I hide behind him.

"Come here now," a soldier yells.

I will not be at the mercy of any more men.

Another shot.

The golden statue, arms slightly outstretched as always, looks pleased to see them. His unchanging expression is one of slightly crushed love, of innocence in the moment of betrayal. With sudden realisation I know we've both been there. The curse of a father's touch.

There is a dreadful creaking, like something being wrenched and yanked away unwillingly. At that moment, the chandelier that hung high in the entrance falls from the ceiling. The crash is devastating. It is not just the stars that have descended, but the very universe itself. The shudder of its impact vibrates through the staircase.

I cower on the steps.

Moments pass. I am still alive.

The floor is a galaxy of cut glass, plaster nebula, and rubble. Chicken Licken, the sky really has fallen in. Except there it is, high above. The fug curls up to meet the morning, clearing the air below. A few clouds are already tinged with the gold of sunrise.

At the bottom of the stairs, *The Midas Boy* now stands, resplendent in the light. He hasn't toppled in the crash or fallen … He's unscathed, inching towards escape. The splayed bodies of crushed soldiers lie in supplication at his feet.

As if the statue walked down the staircase in measured paces on alternate steps, a golden footprint remains in his wake. I have heard of golden letters falling to Earth from Heaven, but nothing so secular. I kneel to touch the metallic print, and as my fingertips come up, coated in warm gold, I'm in awe.

This miracle is something other than Divine, an intervention not of the Creator but, perhaps, the creator of this piece. Sculpture with a soul?

I have to help him.

"Wait here," I tell the gleaming boy, perhaps redundantly, perhaps not.

I run out onto the deserted streets, but the carnage there brings me up short. He's given me another dawn, and I'm determined not to squander this second chance. In the light of day, the task seems impossible. Where will I find a cart and enough volunteers to lift him in this decimated city? Perhaps I can coax him, however mysteriously, to follow me to the convent?

I duck back into the library to speak to him, as silly as that sounds. My words catch in my throat as I realise I'm alone. Of course.

He's gone, just a pool of light shining on two golden footprints that fade in the summer sun.

*

AUTHOR'S NOTE:

The Rape of Belgium is the historical term given to the German invasion and occupation of Belgium from 1914 to 1918. Troops arrived in the city of Louvain on August 19th. It wasn't until the night of August 25th that over two thousand buildings were razed, including the Catholic University's library, destroying some 300,000 books and manuscripts. 248 residents of the city were killed and the rest displaced. German forces insisted the reprisals came after shots were fired on their troops, although this may have been a case of "friendly fire".

MORGAN MELHUISH (he/him) is a queer writer and educator from West Sussex, UK. You can find his stories in The Next Wave *and* Brenda and Effie: A Treasury, *and poetry in places such as* Impossible Archetype, Rabid Oak *and* Outcast. *He lurks on Twitter @mmorethanapage and is currently working on further appearances of a certain golden statue ... !*

JULIET, JULIET

S.J. Townend

I live in a well.

The advert described our one bedroom flat as *designer compartment living*; *the perfect starter home for a professional couple.* But without you here, it feels like a smoke-filled well; a place where light is swallowed.

The ket's ready.

I've cooked it up dry on a plate over the pan we used to cook our chilli in. You'd chop the vegetables and, with the pestle and mortar we bought somewhere deep in the souqs of Tangier, I'd grind the coriander seeds, the cumin, enough chilli to give anyone else but you and I a stomach ulcer. The stone set had been ridiculously heavy, but you said you wouldn't leave without it, so I carried it in my rucksack for you for the last part of our travels. Now, there is no more you, no us, there is no more chilli. Microwave dinners for months. I'm eating trash. Not that I've a hunger since you left. Not for food, anyway.

I've always used something. As a teen, I drank heavily to numb desire, to keep me in a safety net of denial. Then, when I knew for sure I couldn't ever go with a man, I used to numb the rejection from

166

my family when I came out. They said it was *just a phase*, something I'd grow out of. You said the same about my drug use—until you couldn't handle it anymore.

Corrosive white crystals have replaced you, replaced the hole you ripped in my heart when you left. An almost palpable void has spread through one side of me to the other, and I know no amount of chemical fix, no dubious powders, no street elixir will ever patch it up. Still, I carry on using.

Can't even remember what our final argument was about—me, not taking responsibility for my actions, not behaving like an adult, needing professional addiction therapy? Whatever it was, it hammered the endmost nail in the corpse-coffin of our relationship.

I crush the anhydrous rocks into glassy powder with the melted edge of a store card; a store I can no longer afford now I'm paying all the rent. I'd pay anything to have you back—all the money, all the riches, my soul. What I wouldn't give for another kiss and one more night with you.

Three neat snow-slugs lie on the black plate. When these drugs have worn off, I'll look up from the bottom of the well, at the circle of grey sky forever looming large over the stone-cold gullet I'm trapped in. I'll watch the stars come and go, and none of them will be as bright as you. I'll watch the Rorschach Test of clouds pass, devastated I'll never feel the softness of your skin or hair again. I'll sit in the throat of the well and watch and wait and wait, knowing the only bait that'll lure me out, make me step into that bucket to be hauled up to the surface, is the promise of seeing you again.

I bend forwards, greet the first line as if it were an old friend, then, with a tatty note I'll need for cigarettes later curled up between my thumb and finger, I snort.

Before the inch-worm-lines kick in, and I pass out, dissociate for a couple of hours, I set my phone alarm for 5 p.m. I've work to do this afternoon.

The ket kicks in. Fragments of beautiful, incandescent truth as convincing and as powerful as the love I feel for you flit in and out of my peripheral vision. These hints at the meaning of life then let go, disperse, become fantasy, geometric pattern, sound and feeling, sensations that have never been made or heard by anyone before. In this lost moment, nothing makes sense and time is a forgotten concept. And this is how I need my life to be right now, through this hideous period of grief.

I'm furious with you because you were the one who chose to end it. You closed our front door behind you with everything you own in your flight case, and said, '*it's over*,' null and void.

A fog stretches around my paralysed body. Under the influence of the strangest drug I've ever taken, the spirit of me edges closer to the circumference of the stone gullet of the well that now exists in my front room. Do I jump in? All the reasons why I should descend flood my neurones, but the chemicals start to wear off and all I can see now are

stacks of duplicate novels we were going to read together and the fractured television screen you kicked in rage when I said you'd never be
happy without me.

I'm back on the sofa and my phone alarm is nagging. Time for
work.

Sideways sleet penetrates everything but my raincoat-covered torso
on my walk into work. When I arrive and step inside, the rain continues to pelt down and throw itself at the window. Wet socks, sodden
boots, black-with-water jeans.

I ask Margaret on reception if she minds if I take my clothes off,
hang them on the radiator whilst I work. She finds me clean scrubs to
borrow. I joke with her—even though I feel devoid of humour—and
ask her when I can expect my pay rise. Part-time cleaner to surgical
vet is quite the promotion.

I greet all the caged animals being kept in overnight, dozy from
surgery—there are a few perks to my job—and set to work vacuuming
the floor of the veterinary surgery.

I hoover, I dust, I mop. Margaret's shift is finished. She wants to
get home to her myriad of cats, her inane evening quiz shows. "I still
have the bathroom to finish," I say, so she chucks me the spare keys,
tells me to drop them off tomorrow morning.

I do what I need to do, take a little longer than I should, then set the
alarm, lock up at eight, and make the lonely walk home.

*

I rack up my chemical dinner on the plate you used to serve nut-loaf on, and waste more time in another place, a place where time is a forgotten concept and the smell and softness of your hair is near tangible. I wish you were here. I pass out for the night on the sofa.

The next day, mid-morning, I slip on my trainers and wait for the rain to stop. In an opportune moment, I head towards the surgery. I need to return the keys I'm not supposed to have. I wish it were raining again—precipitation would disguise my tear-streaked face.

At the traffic lights, I contemplate whether to chance it and ignore the red suggestion of the signal, when I see you, your hip-length blonde braid. You call it your 'Disney ladder' and it is bouncing behind you. I see your vine tattoo creeping up from the outside of your wrist that matches mine.

It is you. I freeze.

In your hand is a familiar gold-studded purple lead. A brindle whippet of sorts, Berry I think, is on the end of it. The dog is following you, walking to heel. Berry is a regular at the surgery, I saw him there yesterday.

I want to call out 'Juliet', make you turn around, see your face, but your name falls silent on my lips. Saying it aloud will hurt too much. You're in Rio anyway, so I know it can't truly be you—

But the dog—I recognise the distinctive circle patch of raised purple-grey on its flank, in the shape of a round fruit with two leaves and a stem. It is definitely a dog I know. It's definitely Berry. Is it Berry?

"Berry, Berry!" I call the dog's name, quietly and with uncertainty at first, then louder when I'm confident it's him. The handsome mongrel turns and looks at me from across the road, barks and wags his tail in recognition. Then you turn around.

My heart, a caged bird, bashes in my throat.

"Juliet?" I manage, my voice reedy, weak, like the connection between my soul and my physical body when I'm under the influence. The last of my adrenaline quicksilvers through my veins.

"No," you say. Your voice is filled, most oddly, with susurration, but it *is* you—or at least, the very mirror of you. "Now is not our time."

I don't understand. All I know is that I'm a broken mirror. My life is nothing but bad luck and if the shards of my existence were to jab into my heart, I'm certain I'd bleed out black blood, emptiness, and chemicals.

You look at me. Your face is full of sadness. You're never sad. Even when we split, you were sunshine through the rain. Your eyes catch mine, and the exchange feels like a million syncopated firecrackers exploding in my heart. For a nanosecond, I'm stunned and unable to think or move or breathe. Then you continue on your way.

'Please, stop,' I manage to call out. A bus with an advert for panto at the Hippodrome Theatre whizzes past—Widow Twankey, Prince Charming, Cinderella, and ten or so miserable commuters come between us, and then you're gone.

*

I'm clearly distressed when I arrive at the surgery, and I drop the keys on Margaret's desk without a word.

"You alright, chick?" she pipes, her face bright with cheap cosmetics. Some people are eternally cheerful, like Margaret, like you. You were always smiling. Except just then, walking the dog—you weren't smiling then. Your expression said your thoughts were a galaxy away.

"I . . . I . . . just saw someone." I want to tell Margaret I've seen you, but I know you're not in the country and why would you be walking Berry? You don't work where I work. You don't really even like animals.

"Yes chick? Who was that then? Look like you need a cuppa."

I decide to keep my tumbling sanity to myself. If I tell Margaret who, what I've seen, she'll declare me positively unhinged. I can't afford to be signed off sick. Besides, work provides too many bonuses.

"Berry. I just saw Berry. He looks well. Mark works miracles, doesn't he?" I say. How easy we spurt rhetoric, even when we are but a shell.

Margaret's jolly face drops. "Berry, love? Can't have been Berry. Poor thing passed away twenty minutes ago in surgery." She raises her finger and points to the annex, a room to the side of reception where private conversations happen and bad news is given. From it, I hear the sound of sobbing and tissues being pulled from a box. "Owners are in there."

I must've been mistaken—but it was you and I've never been more certain of anything.

I leave without a word, without offering my condolences, without replying when Margaret reminds me of the meeting Mark, the practice manager, has called for all staff tomorrow morning.

It is evening and I'm at work again, this time to clean. I'm plodding along as slowly as I can get away with. Partly because I'm in physical pain and partly because I have things I need to do that require time at the surgery alone. I've learnt how to be less efficient.

My bladder is griping, filtering razorblades from my body fluids, and I can hardly bear the constant burning feeling, this constant urge to pee. They say ket does this to you, when you use for too long, when you're no longer abusing it, but instead, it's abusing you.

"Margaret," I say, "I'm sorry. Don't know what's up with me at the moment. The bathroom is taking me so much longer to do tonight." I fold over slightly, my spine a dowager's hump as I grasp and palpate my sides—where my kidneys are—hoping the pressure of fingertips will ease the congestion, the agony I'm feeling there today.

Margaret smiles at me and I prepare myself to lie to her again, say I'm going to need a little longer. Would she mind *ever so much* leaving me the keys again? I can drop them off tomorrow morning, when we're all in for the meeting?

But before I start my fabrication, she tells me I have to finish on time tonight.

"Rommy, love," —Rommy, short for Romea. No-one calls me Romea.— "Mark's said you need to leave when I do. For health and safety reasons."

I sigh. I'm frustrated. It's never been a problem before. I've been staying late a couple of times a week for a while now.

"Oh," I reply and pause and think and panic slightly. "Best get back to it then. I'll scrub a little faster." I'm mumbling, but Margaret doesn't heat me. She's gone upstairs to carry on with her admin.

It's dark outside now and the animals are being noisier than normal. I put it down to the bad weather and the ones that have been operated on; their anaesthetic starts to wear off about this time. The ones who've been really poorly are waking up, realising they're missing their testes or a limb or the tip of a tail. I hear the surgery door open, even though the practice is closed for business, so I turn around.

The room falls silent.

I drop the disinfectant spray to the floor, clutch my hands to my chest.

Here you are, again.

It's you, but your eyes are dark, your face sad.

"Juliet!" I say.

You've come back for me! You must've changed your mind. My heart is racing and I feel ecstatic but I panic—have I left the frying pan out at home, covered in a thick frosting of ketamine? You'll hit the ceiling if you see it. If you're coming back home. Please, please say you're coming back home. I'm fed up of living down this smoke-filled well alone.

"No," you say. You look at me. A red tear rolls down your face. I feel my heart miss a beat, my own blood sinking to my toes. My face, in shock at the sight of your eyes bleeding, turns wan-white, like yours.

"Your face—" I start. I want to hug you, wipe your tears of blood away, but also, an existential dread like I've never felt before, even in the darkest of my trips, washes over me. The ground is tessellating. Each tile of easy-clean medical laminate flooring is tearing up and dropping down beneath us, into a pit of black.

"No," you say again. "I am not Juliet. I am the light that comes before the dark."

My heart thuds in my throat. You shed another vermillion tear and I freeze. My spine is pressed up against the wall; the wall feels like an iceberg through the thinness of my top. I've no choice but to stand rooted and watch you edge towards the bottom row of post-surgical cages. You crouch down; all the while, rivulets of red are trailing down you, behind you, weaving and flowing into each other, into a thick, wide, deep river of blood.

You reach and open the cage in which Mrs Potter's Siamese cat, Charles, is resting after a tumour was removed from his bowels earlier today.

You pick Charles up in your arms, stroke him. His eyes slowly close and open, his head tilts back in pleasure. You tickle the underneath of his chin and I watch as you almost smile.

"What the—?" I try to speak. My legs are trembling. I press against the wall, it pushes back, thank God. The wall is the only thing keeping me from collapsing with love or fear or both. "If you're not Juliet—who . . . what are you?"

"I am the beginning of the end. I am busy. I am needed in one hundred different places with each minute of your living time that ticks by."

"What? I don't understand. What are you doing with the cat? With Charles? Why are you bleeding? Why aren't you making any sense?" I'm crying too, although my tears are of the see-through variety.

Am I trapped in a nightmare? Tripping? I haven't had a hit, snorted anything yet today—was trying to wait until after my shift. "Why are you saying you're not Juliet?" I wail. Insanity chips at the edge of my thoughts and I promise myself: No. More. Drugs. No more drugs—after I've finished the stash I've accumulated at home.

"At the beginning of your end, you see the one you love the most, the one you trust. When your time ends, you choose who leads you to the other side, you choose who takes you over the bridge. Who will I appear as? Who leads you on your final journey? The one you have loved the most."

My heart can't take this stress, this distorted reality.

You, or this apparition of you, bring the cat up to your lips and kiss him on his head. I see your rose-stained lips drain to a shade as blue as a bruise. I watch you leave in silence, wading through your own river of blood. You take Charles with you. He is calmly embraced in your arms.

Your words crash around in my head, ships in a storm, destroying me, ripping at my last threads of sanity.

The door closes behind you and I watch this form of you pass through the wintered-dandelion seed orb-glow of a dim streetlamp, step past merlons of cityscape moonlight, meld with the darkness of the night, until you're gone. I stagger towards the reception desk, vomit with shock and neglected health, and pass out.

"Rommy! Darling girl, darling girl. What's wrong? You're really not well are you?" Margaret is stroking my hair away from my face and I realise I've been out cold for nearly half an hour. I can smell and taste sick. I pull my sack of bones into a seated position, and notice for the first time how my ribs and hips jut out now like a broken umbrella. I start to apologise for the mess I've made.

"I'm sorry. I . . . I . . . I saw someone, something . . . "

Margaret passes me a towel, tells me to wipe the sick from my clothes. I stare on as she clears up the mess I've made on the floor.

"Is it Charles? Did the sight of Charles do this to you? Lovely cat, wasn't he? Mrs Potter's going to be devastated." Margaret says as she scrubs.

I look at the cage from which Juliet, or Not-Juliet, took out and away the old cat, expecting it to be empty, but there he is: milky eyes, dead opals. His body is arranged in a peculiar curled position. His bandages are soaked through; red. The bottom half of his poor body is swimming in a crimson puddle, his paws are covered in the same sticky vermillion fluid. Charle's lifeless body is still soft, not yet in a state of full rigor mortis.

"It's a frightful shame when they wake and open up their stitches before a solid clot has formed. He bled out. Quite quickly by the looks.

He was fine earlier. I checked on him before I went upstairs." Margaret's eyes are dry but soft. Mine are filling up with tears again.

"You need a break, chick. Get the doctor to sign you off for a bit. I can lend you some money for rent, drop you over some lasagne. You don't seem well, Rommy. And you don't look well," Margaret and her good intentions pause for air. "When was the last time you ate a proper home-cooked meal?"

It's all too much. I know she means well, but I need to get out of here. I need to figure out what's going on. I want to be in your arms, Juliet, but I also want to throw myself into the pan, into a sea of white powder. I want to fall down the well.

From somewhere deep within my bones I summon enough energy to tell Margaret, "I'm fine, just need some sleep."

I grab my bag and start to launch out of the surgery when she calls after me, says she needs to offer me a word of warning.

'Look, listen love—the meeting tomorrow. You need to be there. Make sure you do get a good nights' sleep. Mark knows it's you, chick." She places a caring hand on my arm. I pull away like I've touched the orange hob. "He knows it's you who's been taking the medications, the tranquilisers, the barbiturates, all the Class A's, from the locked cabinet. He's going to confront you tomorrow in front of everyone. Time to come clean, love. Time to *get* clean. We're all here for you, to help."

I bolt out of the door, run all the way home. There's no way I'll be going back in the morning. I want nothing more to do with the place.

Full of rivers of blood, full of haunted versions of you—I can't be surrounded by death anymore. But I am surrounded by death. All I can think of is death. Death, and you.

Why are you torturing my mind, my soul like this, Juliet? Why do I keep seeing you leading dead animals away?

Back at home, in the pit of a well, I put on a final cook. I need this cook. I collapse back on my sofa and wait for the flat to be thick with the pungent, caustic, soapy stench of ketamine.

I'm going to take it all: several grams, and the crushed contents of a half-full bottle of pills I found in the locked cupboard. I long to see her again: Juliet, or Not-Juliet, the creature of beauty with the Disney braid, the vine tattoo, the red tears; the girl with the same face and voice as you. I will let her take my hand, kiss my lips, carry my frail, exhausted body in her arms from the light which screams out in nothing but grey for me, and on, into the noiseless dark.

I crush and swipe and stretch the crystals into lines this last time, taking pride in how it's all laid out. With many white lines, I draw your face. I eke the powder round into curves, semi-circles, ovals, waves, and create an image in your likeness. I curve round the thickest white line to form the tip of your patrician nose. Pressing white grains into almond shapes, I form your beautiful eyes. Weaving white lines around the edge of the plate with the tip of the card, I form the long braid in which you always keep your hair.

You.

I roll my note and push it hard up into a sore, weeping nostril, and then inhale every last grain of you, and, once more, fall back into the well of my sofa.

A blanket of bliss rolls over me with a sigh like fog on the moors. Peace spreads out from my core to my tips.

But then, my heart rate shoots up and then plummets back down, dropping away to nothing. Consciousness slips into a cloud of smoke, all the shade of you, and I step over the edge and allow myself to fall. My eyes, beetle-black, open up as I reach the pit of the well. There you are. You are sad again, my Juliet, or my Not-Juliet, or this angel-of-death version of you who never raises a smile.

You say nothing, but reach out a willowy arm. I see your vine tattoo. We both got one done for your twenty-fifth birthday. Yours starts at your wrist and twists and twirls all the way up your outstretched arm to the top of your smooth shoulder. Mine is similar, a continuation, but extends a little further around my neck to where I like to be kissed the most. I take hold of your hand, and you pull me in. Your arm of vines reels me, wraps me up in the softest, most brilliant feeling. Warm yet cool, safe yet unknown. I am next to you again, or this version of you, Juliet-Not-Juliet.

And then I let you kiss me. Your lips taste of Saturdays and of what I can only imagine heaven is like if heaven were to exist. This is the start of my long goodbye.

I am one thousand candles, all lit up at once, and then I am those same one thousand candles, all blown out in unison. I let you take me from the light which is becoming grey, is becoming more grey by the second. I realise time means nothing anymore, and now, like Berry, like Charles, I have reached my destination and I have become nothingness in the dark. I know now that you, Juliet-Not-Juliet, are not human. You are, in fact, Death. And now, so am I.

*

The stench of rotten flesh and ketamine can be smelt by them all from the stairwell. Juliet hammers at the apartment door for ten minutes until the firefighters insist their way in is quicker, and they haven't time to waste. Juliet steps back, fearing the worst. She changed her mind, decided she's still in love with Rommy. She raced home as soon as her flight landed. She can't wait to see her girl, her Rommy. Can't wait to forgive her and take her back.

Juliet strokes the tip of her long braid up and down her inner arm, tracing the outline of the vine running up it, while she waits for the rescue team to batter down the door.

Juliet will forgive the drug taking, she is going to help Rommy get the professional help she needs. They'll escape the powerful trap of addiction together, the right way this time, with help and support, not alone. In time, Juliet knows things can be what they once were. Good again.

But Juliet knows in her heart it's too late. She knows the dark room that is about to be opened up before them all is the beating heart of the corridor stench, but within that room, the flat in which she and

Rommy used to be so happy, she knows there will be no actual beating hearts.

The door is down. The slam of it hitting the floor is nothing compared to the implosion Juliet feels in the pit of her stomach, or the crush she takes in the chest, two planets colliding. She rushes over and sees her love, her Rommy, flat out on her back on the sofa. A thick ring of dried white residue is around her nose, a powder-encrusted plate; a rolled note both lie just inches from her dead, unfurled fingertips. A mottled patch of dry vomit mats her precious girl's face and hair to the fabric of the sofa. Rommy's cheeks, Rommy's bare stomach, the space between her thighs—are all vomiting with maggots. The busy vortex of flies moving in Brownian motion above Rommy's dishevelled, stiff body is too much. The sight and the smell of her is too much. Too strong.

Juliet's loss is too great.

"I'm afraid she's gone," a crouched fire-fighter with kindness and concern in his eyes says to Juliet. "Is there anyone we can call?"

But Juliet is struck dumb with grief and then, she too, is gone.

She runs down the stairs of the apartment complex, as speedy as a stone dropping down a well; needs to be out of the building, far away from the memories, the dead body of her lover, the stench of death and ketamine.

Juliet wipes tears from her eyes. They are clear tears, salty tears, tears of the living, not tears of blood. The brightness of the outside world jabs at her eyes like pins.

For a fleeting second, Juliet sees her lover, sees Rommy with an arm extended, with her matching vine tattoo snaking up her arm. She sees Rommy's other hand pointing at her own neck, to the end of her vine, where she likes to be kissed the most. But where the ink of Rommy's tattoo had once been green, now the vines are black, toxic, throbbing; as if close to bursting open through her near-translucent skin.

"Juliet, Juliet," Rommy-Not-Rommy with the sad, dark eyes calls out. "Let me lead you from the light into the dark."

Juliet swears she's just seen her lover Rommy lifeless, lost forever down the infinite, bleak well of drugs and sickness. But here, outside, Rommy is beckoning her closer, calling to her for an embrace, one more passionate kiss—but Juliet only sees Rommy, and does not see the speeding truck as she steps out into the road.

And Juliet's light, too, is extinguished.

S.J. TOWNEND writes horror, sci-fi, and dark fiction and is currently pulling together her first collection of short stories, working title: Sick Girl Screams. *She has short stories published with Ghost Orchid Press, Gravestone Press, and* Gravely Unusual Magazine, *and has self-published two dark mystery novels, which are both available on Amazon. You can find her on Twitter: @SJTownend.*

A WOUND FULL OF TEETH

Sam Kyung Yoo

The cashier is staring at her.

Mai just wants to buy this one massive plastic tub of peanut butter-filled pretzels and a bag of apples. Normally she would go through self-checkout, but all the machines are undergoing maintenance.

The blonde woman ahead of her in line has a cart stocked high with every food group. The cashier scans each item with practiced ease, his movements fluid and quick as if on autopilot. He doesn't say much to the woman beyond the standard greeting and pleasantries. Instead, he keeps turning to glance at Mai.

Mai touches a hand to the back of her head, confirming that the hood of her sweatshirt is still securely in place. She tugs on the brim, pulling it down further over her head.

The cashier finishes ringing the blonde woman up. Mai places her items on the conveyor belt and gets out her wallet.

The cashier sets the bag of apples on the scale and types in the PLU code one agonizingly slow key stroke at a time. Mai keeps her eyes down. His name tag reads, "Michael, employee for eight years."

"So, what are you?" he says.

She feels the teeth in the back of her head click together. She breathes in, plastering a polite smile on her face.

"I'm sorry?" she says.

"What are you?" he repeats. His eyes are a light blue, making his gaze seem even more piercing.

Her pulse pounds in her ears along with the muted clicking of chattering teeth.

He adds, "Like, what country are you from, originally?"

Mai stares at him, uncomprehending, before the tension in her chest eases. This is well-traveled territory. This is something she can handle.

"I'm American, actually," she says with a smile, as if he's asked such an interesting and charming question.

"But where were you born?" he says.

"Right here, in California," she says.

"Okay, but where are your parents from?"

She laughs like they're both in on a good joke. "Also California."

"But where are you really from?" he insists. "Like, what are you biologically?"

He's getting frustrated now, as if he doesn't get why she won't just hurry up and tell him the answer he wants to hear. Sometimes it's worth it to keep going, just to prove a point, but she's hungry and still has work to do today.

"Japanese," she says. It feels like conceding defeat. But she isn't supposed to put up a fight anyway.

His face lights up. He looks her over again, appraising her. "Oh yeah, you know, I could kind of tell."

She stares back at him, taking in his white skin and light brown hair and she thinks it must be nice to look like a "real" American. Like the blonde woman who had been ahead of her in line.

Teeth grind together in the back of her head, muffled by the thick fabric of her hood. She keeps smiling as he finally scans the tub of pretzels.

"Sa-ya-nor-ah," he grins, handing her the receipt.

"Thank you," she says.

The story goes, there once was a woman who did not eat anything.

Her husband was rich, but selfish. He despised spending money on anything that wasn't for himself and resented having to feed her. So she ate as little as possible and never asked for anything. She was a hard worker, and never complained.

One day though, the little she did require got to be too much for him, and his patience wore out. So he buried an ax in the back of her head.

But she survived.

The man could not finish the deed and still claim it as an accident, so he lied, and praised her recovery as a miracle. She had not seen anything, for he had come at her from behind, and she could not seem to remember anything about what had really happened that day.

The wound, however, did not heal.

Inside of the gash on the back of her skull grew teeth, a tongue, and a hunger that demanded to be fed.

She ate through his stores of rice. She ate his servants. And in the end, she devoured him as well.

The story makes it sound like this was a punishment brought down upon the man for his excessive parsimony, but Mai never understood why the woman was the one who had to be so hideously transformed. It didn't seem fair. It also didn't seem fair for it to become a hereditary curse, passed down through the woman's bloodline.

Mai wonders just who is being punished here.

As Mai drives back to her apartment from the grocery store, the second mouth in the back of her head lets out a guttural snarl, teeth bared. The growling sends vibrations throughout her skull.

"You have to calm down," she says as she flicks her turn signal on.

The story goes, a young female hiker was walking down Badger Trail when a figure in white appeared on the path ahead, seemingly out of nowhere. When the hiker moved closer, the mysterious figure turned their head and she saw they had no eyes, nose, or mouth—the front of their head was just a smooth surface of blank, featureless skin.

The hiker died a couple days later of a heart attack.

"So based on that description, it being a dalgyal gwishin seems more likely," Syd narrates as they walk down the trail path. "Like I said before, noppera-bou are pranksters, and I genuinely can't recall any report of a noppera-bou actually killing a human. Meanwhile, people that meet dalgyal gwishin almost always end up falling ill and dying shortly after."

Mai matches pace with Syd, moving backwards while keeping the video camera steady on them as they continue talking.

"At the same time, the hiker had an underlying heart issue," Syd says. "It's possible she had a run-in with a noppera-bou and the stress exacerbated her condition, or her heart attack was from completely natural causes, and it was just a coincidence."

Mai's lips twitch into a smile. Though Syd labels themself as a ghost hunter in their YouTube channel description, their videos aren't about searching for evidence of ghosts. They act more like a wildlife filmmaker. When the two of them go to locations to film like this, Syd treats it as an opportunity to get footage of an apparition in its natural habitat, or in this case, a chance to properly identify the "species." To them, the existence of spirits and apparitions is already a given.

Mai looks over Syd's shoulder at the faceless figure in white standing in the middle of the trail path behind them, about thirty paces away.

In this case, Syd is right.

The dalgyal gwishin remains eerily still. Mai doesn't know how something can stare without eyes, but she knows it's looking at Syd.

"Also—sorry, this is a tangent," Syd breaks eye contact with the camera lens to look at Mai. "So, if a dalgyal gwishin is the result of someone who died without any loved ones or family to perform death rites for them, which is based specifically in Korean culture and spirituality, could a Korean American become one after they died? I can imagine Korean immigrants would, but what if you're second gen, or third—"

Syd trips on a pebble. Their arms windmill frantically before they manage to get their feet back under them. They keep their arms out-stretched for a moment, looking a bit like a gymnast who managed to stick the landing purely by accident.

"You can't tell, but Mai is laughing at my suffering," Syd says to the camera, and to the future viewers. They are well aware that Mai is going to include this whole bit in the episode.

Mai's snickering is too quiet to be picked up by any of the microphones. She tilts her head to one side, raising an eyebrow at them.

Syd jabs an accusing finger at her. "Say something. Let the people know you're real, you coward," they whisper-shout.

Mai snorts.

There's a popular fan conspiracy theory that "Mai Futaguchi" is just a figment of Syd Yang's imagination since Mai's existence has never been confirmed visibly or audibly in a video. Even when faced with practical responses like, "Then who's holding the camera?" many viewers still like to refer to Mai as "the channel cryptid." It's become a running joke at this point.

"How do you walk backwards so gracefully anyway?" Syd complains. "It's like you've got eyes on the back of your head."

Mai's jaw involuntarily clenches for a moment before she forces herself to relax and smile. "You caught me," she says. She wishes she had a free hand to tug down on the brim of her hood. "You want to start from the beginning of this segment again?" Mai continues in a lighter tone. "We still have to finish recording."

Syd blinks. "Oh yeah. Shit, what was I talking about?"

"If a third gen Korean American could become a dalgyal gwishin," Mai says.

"Right. Okay, so … "

Syd alternates between trying to make eye contact with the camera lens while they talk, and glancing down at the ground to make sure they don't trip on anything else. Mai continues to walk backwards without any issue.

But no matter how far they go, the faceless figure on the path behind Syd never gets any farther away, even though Mai doesn't see it take a single step.

Teeth chatter restlessly in the back of Mai's head. Her hair coils and shifts inside her hood.

At first, when Mai was born, she was normal. That's how it always is.

Then one day, she felt a snapping sound from deep inside her skull as the back of her head split open and grew teeth. She could feel a second pair of lips in the back of her head, new monstrous teeth chewing on the bottommost lip and a guttural growling that reverberated through her bones.

Mai's mother gently combed her fingers through Mai's hair, parting it to take a closer look at the newly formed mouth that was still jabbering and spitting.

"Shhh," her mother soothed. At the same time, the mouth on the back of her mother's head made a sound like a hissing snake.

Mai's second mouth calmed.

"You have to learn how to stay quiet," her mother said, stroking Mai's hair. "That's how you keep yourself safe."

Syd sprawls across the foot of the king-sized motel room bed. "Why do we still have more filming to do?" they moan at the ceiling.

Mai looks up from where she is laying out all the equipment they'll need for when they go back to Badger Trail tonight.

"You could stay here and sleep," she offers. "I'm fine with going to record the footage by myself."

Syd grunts.

"You wouldn't be missing anything exciting," Mai insists.

"Not with that attitude." Syd points finger guns at her, or at least they try to. Their aim is off by a significant margin due to their eyes being closed. This doesn't surprise Mai. Syd's night owl sleep schedule and frequent late-night research binges make them very incompatible with early mornings like the one they had today.

"You should sleep at least for a bit. We still have a couple of hours before we head out again," Mai says. Syd groans, mashing the heels of their palms into their eye sockets. "And if the goal is to stay awake, I don't think popping your eyeballs is going to help."

Syd drags their hands down their face. "Did you know pressure on your eyeballs can lower your heart rate by twenty percent? Because

191

of the oculocardiac reflex. Vagus nerve." Their words come out slurred, sleepiness making them sound drunk.

Mai snorts and returns her attention to uncoiling the thermal camera's charging cable. "I'm going to interpret that as you agreeing to take a nap."

Syd heaves a sigh. "Wake me up when it's time to head out?"

"Of course."

Mai waits for Syd's breathing to slow down and even out before she goes over to pull the top layer blanket of the bed covers back, draping it over them.

She finishes her inventory of all the filming equipment, double-checking that every device is properly plugged in and charging.

Then, she heads out and drives back to Badger Trail.

Mai stands in the middle of the path.

The faceless figure walks toward her.

She can't help but try and make eye contact with where the eyes should be, but the front of the ghost's head is smooth and blank, like a sheet of skin that has been stretched over the surface of an egg.

With no one to remember or honor them, the ghost eroded, losing its face and sense of self. All that's left is this empty, lonely maw that feeds on the lives of anyone it encounters—unwitting hikers just passing by, or someone like Syd.

Tendrils of Mai's hair slither out from the inside of her hood, pushing it back until it slips off her head. The hair twines like snakes, writhing and coiling in the air just in front of her.

The mouth in the back of her head snarls, "You can't have them."

The night sky above Badger Trail is clear as glass, the stars and the moon bathing the world in a soft silvery glow that is just bright enough to see by.

Syd records POV footage with the thermal camera while Mai films with the night vision camcorder. They go back and forth along the path, but the faceless ghost does not make an appearance. Syd ruefully calls it a night after the fourth circuit.

"Considering you're someone who actually believes supernatural beings are real, you have no sense of danger," Mai says as they walk back to the car. "You're like an Arctic wildlife expert that keeps going up to polar bears to try and give them a high-five."

Syd bursts out laughing. "Maybe give me a bit more credit than that," they say.

"If it *had* been a dalgyal gwishin, you would've died," Mai points out. "But you never get even a little bit scared."

Syd shrugs, smiling at her. "I have you with me. You make me feel brave."

Mai doesn't have a response to that, overcome by a warm all-encompassing fondness.

Mai can feel the light of her laptop screen burning into her tired eyes. The world outside her apartment window is pitch black now, and yet here she is doing her final check of the Waverly Hills Sanatorium episode for what feels like the umpteenth time. She leans back in her desk chair with a groan.

Post-production on this one has already taken her so long; she just wants to upload it and be done, but there's this one section she's second-guessing herself on.

It's a bit of night vision footage from when she and Syd had been exploring the sanatorium's famous "body chute" tunnel. The audio recording is somewhat distorted, every sound in the long dark tunnel echoing.

And then, the mouth in the back of Mai's head imitates the sound of a hoarse, croaking death rattle.

Syd shouts *"No"* at the top of their lungs. The sound quickly overwhelms everything else as it ricochets around the narrow passageway. This is quickly followed by Syd's peals of laughter as they say, "I realize that may or may not have just been a frog."

Mai stares at her laptop screen. It's one of her favorite moments from their time filming. It's not a bad thing, to have it in the episode, she tells herself. She doesn't want to have to cut it.

She uploads the episode.

It's well past five in the morning by the time Mai drags herself into bed. Just as she's settling under the covers, her phone buzzes.

The text from Syd just reads, *Did you know the Ancient Greeks believed early ventriloquists had ghosts in their stomachs?*

The corner of Mai's mouth turns upwards.

Go to sleep, she texts back.

Mai lies on her bed, flat on her stomach. Her phone rests on the blankets beside her face.

"I saw that episode you posted," her mother says, her voice tinny and fractured through the phone's speaker. "You have to be careful. You've been taking more risks lately." The signal is surprisingly decent, considering her mother is calling from the edge of the grid in the middle of nowhere.

"I know," Mai mumbles. Tendrils of her hair snake their way down to the opened tub of peanut butter-filled pretzels that's sitting on the floor beside her bed, snagging another mouthful of pretzel nuggets to reel in and drop into the chomping teeth of her second mouth.

"You can never know how someone will react when they find out," her mother warns. "Not until it's too late to take it back."

The teeth in the back of Mai's head snap together, pulverizing the pretzels.

"And even if Syd doesn't run away screaming, what if he wants to make a video out of you?" her mother continues. "Imagine the view count on a real-life freak show like that."

Mai cringes. There is a bitter edge to her mother's voice that Mai knows isn't directed at her, but the words sting as they cut into her nonetheless.

"They," Mai corrects softly. "It's 'what if *they* want to make a video' out of me."

Her mother just sighs.

"And Syd wouldn't do that," Mai argues. "They're a good person, Mom."

Countless viewers have clamored for a face reveal of "the channel cryptid," wheedling for visual confirmation of Mai. Syd ignores these, always firmly respecting Mai's boundaries.

Her mother doesn't say anything for a moment. "Are you in love with them?" she says.

Mai hasn't given much thought to relationships. She's never seen the need, since she doesn't want anything physically intimate. Syd is just her favorite person in the entire world. She doesn't need to ask them out or kiss them in the rain, she just wants to be with them always, for as long as they'll have her.

"When I told your father, he said it didn't matter and that he loved me anyway," her mother says. "And I don't think he was lying. I think he really did love me back. It just wasn't enough, in the end. Not when we had you. Because you were perfect. Such a beautiful baby, and he loved you so much. I think that's why he couldn't handle it when you changed. Even though I told him it would happen. He just couldn't bear to look at you anymore."

Mai remembers. It was a quiet, understated fracture. Her father silently accepted a job position in Sweden. He didn't file for a divorce. He kept supporting them as his family.

But he doesn't speak to either of them anymore.

"If only we could eat memories," her mother muses. "Like how the baku can eat people's dreams. Living with other people wouldn't be so scary that way."

But it's lonely, Mai wants to say. It's so lonely to never be known. To never be seen. To never feel like another human being would accept you if they really knew you. She can't live like her mother, living out in a secluded homestead surrounded by acres of wilderness and not a neighbor in sight for miles.

Mai loves people, and Syd makes her feel like she's home. She wants to believe it would be okay. But she can see the nightmare and how it would unfold. She imagines the look on Syd's face, shock, terror, disgust—

The mouth on the back of her head lets out an anguished, keening sound.

The Rocky Springs Mine, also called The Wailing Mine, is an abandoned remnant of the area's early coal mining industry.

The story goes, back in the 1880s, three white miners attacked a Chinese miner named Liang Chin, bludgeoning him with a shovel repeatedly until Liang Chin's skull cracked open. Then, they dragged him into the mine to drop his body down a mine shaft.

"But it turned out that Liang Chin wasn't dead yet," Syd narrates as they walk down the tunnel. "Somehow, he was able to grab onto one of his assailants and took him down with him when he fell."

Their helmet's head lamp is switched off for the time being while Mai films them so as not to interfere with the video camera's auto exposure. They're relying solely on Mai's head lamp to illuminate them for the shot.

"Good for him," Mai mutters. She'll have to cut that bit of audio out in post, but she means it, with all her heart.

"Okay, but actually though, can we end this segment here?" Syd says. "I can barely remember my script while I'm worrying about whether you're going to walk backwards into a concealed mine shaft or something."

"Then we can leave an exciting note for future explorers: 'warning, pit fall ahead,'" Mai says.

The Wailing Mine is a popular site for the more daring ghost hunters and tourists. Its walls are riddled with useful graffiti indicating things like which tunnels lead to dead ends or which areas are the easiest to traverse. The path they're on right now is consistently well-traveled and has actually seen some professional maintenance over the years.

"It'd still be a stupid way for you to die! You're not even wearing your helmet right," Syd yells.

Mai is aware that wearing her safety helmet on top of her hood with the chin strap unbuckled is an affront to all safety measures. She mostly has it on for the sake of video lighting, and an attempt at giving Syd some peace of mind that has clearly not worked.

The mouth in the back of her head sighs quietly and Mai resists the urge to do the same—the air in here is somewhat stifling.

"It doesn't help that behind you is just Absolute Darkness," Syd moans. "My eyes haven't adjusted at all because I've been looking straight into your head lamp. It's so scary, Mai. I'm losing my mind."

Mai laughs, lowering her video camera. "Okay, okay. I'll stop."

"*Thank you*," Syd says. They stop walking to switch their helmet's light on.

Mai moves to stand beside them. “The acoustics in here aren’t ideal anyway. You’ll probably want to record separate voice over narration later,” she says.

“Cool,” Syd drawls. “So I can go ahead and switch this mic off and complain freely about what a nightmare this place is every step of the way.”

“I can hold your hand if you want,” Mai offers.

Syd shoots her a half-glare, half-pout. “Don’t patronize me,” they grumble.

Mai snickers, leaning into them and nudging her shoulder against theirs. She was only half-joking, but their petulant expression is still perfect.

They set out again, this time walking side by side.

The path to the mine shaft Liang Chin was thrown into is marked with bright white arrows. It’s the primary destination of all visitors, since most believe it to be the source of the wailing sounds. The plan is to shoot another segment of Syd once they get there.

In the meantime, Mai intermittently captures POV footage of their forward progress to serve as visuals for the video to accompany Syd’s voice over.

“You know, I still can’t get over how easily the other two miners got away with it,” Syd muses as they walk. “They told the authorities that Liang Chin was the sole aggressor and people believed them, just like that.”

The teeth in the back of Mai's head clench so tightly she can feel her skull creaking. "Of course," she says. She keeps her tone light, though she feels slightly nauseous.

"Research for this video sucked," Syd says gloomily. "Let's go to Hawaii for the next episode. They have noppera-bou there for sure."

This draws a huff of laughter from Mai. It's weak, but a welcome relief. Her chest has been feeling tight for a little while now.

Then she hears it.

The wailing.

They've been to haunted locations before and recorded sounds that have toed the knife's edge between "just the wind" and the sound of something more. But not this time. This is the sound of a man's voice in agony.

Mai turns to Syd and sees in their wide eyes and blanched face that they hear it too.

"What is that?" Syd whispers.

Underneath the wailing is the echo of staggering, labored footsteps, and the sound of something heavy being dragged on the ground.

Mai had felt a hint of unease when they first entered this mine, but it had seemed negligible. The nausea had kept building, but in equally negligible increments. It crept up on her, like the metaphorical pot of water slowly heating up around the oblivious frog sitting inside until it boiled.

Only now does she realize the suffocating pressure had been a territorial display, an aggressive signal for her to back off. And she'd ignored it, thoughtlessly marching straight into the heart of this place.

A sharp hiss strains through the gritted teeth in the back of her head.

"Get behind me," Mai commands. "And start backing up towards the entrance."

Mai turns back to the impenetrable dark of the tunnel ahead and sets the camera bag down beside her. Her hair coils and twists inside her hood, but she is hyper aware of Syd standing behind her. She can only hope that the horrible sounds echoing from the mine around them are loud enough to drown out the sounds of the teeth in the back of her head chattering and gnawing in frustration.

Then Mai hears the cruel impact of metal against flesh, and Syd's cry of pain behind her.

Mai whirls around just in time to see Syd falling to the floor as they are struck by the metal shovel a second time, this time in the back of the head. Mai looks up at what is standing over them.

The two ghosts are tangled together. The white man stands on crooked legs, his shin bones splintered. Liang Chin lies on the ground, his body mangled, his face a bloody, pulpy mess. His spine is crumpled and folded like bent wire, but he still clutches the man's ankle with a vice-like grip.

The white man staggers forward, moaning. With every step, he drags Liang Chin along the ground behind him.

Syd tries to crawl backwards on their hands and feet. Their head is bleeding.

The man lifts the shovel again.

"Don't you fucking touch them," Mai screams twofold, her voice in tandem with the feral shriek of her second mouth.

Her hair tears free from her hood, sending her helmet tumbling off, taking the head lamp with it. She doesn't need it anyway; she can see in the dark just fine. Her hair writhes and unwinds, growing to fill the tunnel around her as she abandons her disguise of seeming small.

The ghost stumbles backward, or at least he tries to.

That's right, she thinks. You should be scared of me. I'll rip you apart.

Her hair surges forward like a horde of snakes. She devours him piecemeal, her second mouth gnashing its teeth in a bottomless hunger. Soon, there is nothing left of the man, and there is no more wailing.

Liang Chin looks up at her from where he now lies alone on the ground. Mai holds out her hand, and she can feel the chill of his touch when he takes it. His ruined body unfolds as he gets to his feet. Now, he stands tall, unbroken and unbloodied. He inclines his head to her. Then he is gone, like dissipating vapor.

The air in the mine is lighter now, but Mai is still not free to breathe. She can feel the light of Syd's head lamp on her, as if it is burning into her skin.

She turns to see Syd leaning against the tunnel wall. Trails of blood drip from their scalp, running down their face. Syd is staring at her.

Mai meets their eyes, feeling brittle and empty. She wants to ask, *Do I still make you feel brave?*

Mai keeps her eyes locked on the road ahead of her as she drives them to the hospital. Tension vibrates down her spine, her skin prickling whenever she senses Syd turning to glance at her. Mai's shoulders are locked in place like she's bracing for an impact.

But Syd doesn't say anything.

When they arrive, Syd tells the hospital staff they fell and slammed the back of their head into a dumpster by accident, which seems to be a sufficiently believable story. The doctor says Syd's head injury doesn't require any stitches but diagnoses them with a mild concussion and instructs them to rest and take it easy before sending them on their way.

The drive back to the motel is equally quiet. The background noise of the road and the clicking turn signal are not enough to mask the hoarse, rattling sound coming from Mai's second mouth.

She hears Syd exhale shakily and tightens her grip on the steering wheel, her knuckles turning bone white.

Once they get back to their motel room, Mai forces herself to speak: "You can shower first." Her voice comes out as a rasp. She clears her throat. "If you want." *To wash off the blood*, she doesn't add. She keeps her eyes on the floor.

"Yeah, okay," Syd says.

Mai listens to the padding of Syd's feet, followed by the sound of the bathroom door closing behind them.

She lets out a shaky exhale. Suddenly her hoodie is too constricting. The stagnant smell of the mine still clings to it, and the bunched-up fabric of the hood is strangling her. She wrenches it off and hurls it into the corner. Only then do the tears spill over.

She covers her face with her hands. She presses the heels of her palms into her eyes and remembers Syd's sleepy ramblings about the oculocardiac reflex. She laughs, but it comes out sounding more like a sob.

She scrubs her face dry and focuses on packing up the filming equipment. They'll be driving back to LA in the morning. She's just finished wrapping up all the cables when she hears Syd cursing from the bathroom.

Mai walks over to the door. Her hand hovers to knock, but she hesitates.

Syd continues to hiss in frustration.

"Are you okay?" Mai asks.

"I'm fine," Syd says through gritted teeth. "Just having some issues with my hair. And scalp."

Mai hesitates. "I could help?"

There is a pause. Before Mai can panic and start to backpedal and apologize, Syd says, "Yeah, sure. Give me a sec."

Mai hears the water shut off. After another couple moments the door opens, and Syd is standing there with a towel wrapped around their waist. Their chest is bare, exposing the top surgery scars that trace across their ribcage in faded silvery lines of long since healed tissue. Their hair is half wet, half dry.

Syd gestures to the back of their head. "The dried blood is just—"

"Right, of course," Mai says.

They awkwardly maneuver around each other in the narrow bathroom until Syd is sitting on the edge of the bathtub, their feet inside.

Mai stands behind them with a hand towel soaked in cold water, gently loosening the clumps of dried blood from Syd's hair.

Even after she's gotten the worst of it, she keeps stroking Syd's hair anyway. She's not ready to let go just yet.

"I knew there was something," Syd says suddenly.

Mai freezes, blood tinted water dripping from her hands.

"Sometimes, you get this look," they say. "You'll go motionless, but your eyes drift, scanning around like you're tracking movement. Like on Badger Trail, I knew something was there because you kept glancing behind me."

The mouth on the back of Mai's head sucks in a breath, which is good because the mouth on her face certainly isn't doing that right now.

"And weird noises happen around us all the time—poltergeists, EVP, whatever—but after a while I realized a lot of the sounds were coming from this one voice. Sort of like how I'd know your voice anywhere, your—" Syd pauses uncertainly. "Your other voice? I started to recognize that too."

Syd turns, swinging their legs out from the tub so they can turn to face her. Teeth click and chatter in the back of Mai's head as Syd meets her eyes.

"I didn't really have any good theories though." They chuckle. "Definitely nothing that came close. But I don't care. You're still the same person. You're still my best friend."

"You don't really mean that," Mai says. "You were terrified. I don't want you to have to lie to me." She can't stand the thought of Syd forcing a smile even while they're scared of her.

She thinks about her father and how he said it didn't matter to him. He said he still loved them, but it just wasn't enough. He never even said goodbye.

"I'd rather you tell me to my face and—" Mai chokes. She doesn't really want that either. She doesn't know what would hurt more or less. Everything feels like it hurts. Her heart aches and creaks under the weight of it all like a battered ship.

"Hey, it's okay," Syd says, standing up.

"No it's not," the mouth on the back of Mai's head says. "You're going to leave."

Syd's eyes widen for a moment. Their brow furrows. "I'm not going to leave you," they say.

"You don't know that," the mouth says. "Maybe you believe it now, but you'll change your mind."

"When your tolerance runs out," Mai finishes, her voice hollow.

Syd steps forward.

They reach for her slowly, giving her the chance to back away or tell them to stop. Mai does neither of these things.

They wrap their arms around her and hold her close.

"I really love you, you know?" Syd says.

Mai's emotions are too big in her chest to articulate.

But the mouth in the back of her head says, "When I'm with you, I feel happier than I ever thought I could be."

It says, "I love you more than anything."

It says, "Please stay. Please stay."

"I'm not going anywhere," Syd says. "You'll always have me. No matter what."

SAM KYUNG YOO is a writer and taekwondo instructor from Massachusetts. When asked, "where are you REALLY from though?" their answer is "technically Germany" since that's where they were born. Their work has appeared in Fireside Magazine, Open Minds Quarterly, Unlocking the Magic *(Cuppatea Publications), and is forthcoming in* The Dead Inside *(Dark Dispatch). You can find them on Twitter @SamKyungYoo.*

FAREWELL HOUSE

Kayla Whittle

Rumors claimed the museum on the hill was closing because it was haunted. In most ways that mattered, the rumors were incorrect. It was less romantic to say the old manor no longer had any funding. Humans weren't creative when it came to hauntings, anyway, thinking the only beings that clung to homes were ghosts.

Whenever the museum emptied and the tall clock behind the check-in desk chimed midnight, the local residents left their paintings. Moonlight pulled through locked windows, and the noise of shoe heels and laughter filled the silence left behind after the last of their guests had gone. Rumors, of course, originated somewhere, and most ghost stories came from the stray curious wanderer, nose pressed close to fogging, cold glass. There had been one or two delayed janitors who'd suddenly found themselves surrounded by living art and just as suddenly decided to find a new occupation.

On most nights, Bea stepped out of her painting. Colors crackling, frame shifting, a smile extended toward the gentleman who offered her a polite hand down. He lived within the canvas next door; not part of her collection, but sometimes she thought that was what she liked best about him. Her own portrait was muted, a background of greenery with hardly any bursting color. Her dress was white, simple—scandalous, by the standards of some of the impressionists down the corridor, and old-fashioned when held up against the guests who came by day. Charles' lines were all bold; red and yellow and orange, though the surrealist who'd dreamed him up had only given detail to half of his body.

"Charles," she nodded, once she had her feet and the polished marble firm beneath her. "How kind of you."

They didn't meet every night, she and the elderly man who'd been painted halfway. Sometimes Charles slept a few hours too late within his frame; sometimes Bea was in too much of a rush to get downstairs to bother with polite conversation. That night was one unlike the others, because it was the last they would spend in the same location.

"I was hoping to help you down tonight. Didn't want to miss you," Charles said. The abstract edge to his face wavered, tendrils of red and orange seeping into the air beside him. Color seethed with the sigh that escaped him as he added, absently, "Beautiful night for it."

On impulse—a stark, panicked moment of remembrance—Bea reached forward to squeeze his hand again. The paint on her cheekbones felt curiously hot; watercolor pooled by her irises.

"It has been my honor and privilege to hang beside you all these years," Bea said. "Saying goodbye is only so bitter when pleasant company forces you to appreciate what you're losing."

"You flatter me, and you know well how I've enjoyed your company since my acquisition," Charles said. It was often a difficult adjustment for any painting, learning a new home. Eternity was frightening when one had no control over it. "But I won't keep you, Beatrice. Please, give Henry my regards."

With regret, Bea left Charles behind. Red and orange dripped from his edges; the droplets scattered across the floor would be gone by morning, sunk deep into the foundations to leave the museum clean and spotless, waiting for humanity. A trail of white followed Bea as she walked away, dress billowing by her ankles, knowing she'd likely never see her dear friend again.

Never see any of them again. She was only guaranteed to stay with her sisters, the rest of her collection. Bea had been painted last and was youngest both in appearance and composition. Sometimes it grated, to always be seventeen, though over the decades her sisters' protective grip had thankfully loosened. Bea passed their empty portraits, bland pastoral scenes. The others were off saying their own goodbyes, giving her some of the space she craved. They would see each other again the next night, and the next, and the next, wherever life and humanity took them. The other collections would likely be housed elsewhere.

Dozens of paintings hung in Bea's gallery alone. Not every resident liked to wander the museum; a boy two floors up, one room over, had slept through the past century. Perhaps that provided a sort of bliss, that ignorance. Those who woke knew their home on the hill was closing for good. The humans had already held their farewell parties, marble spattered with teardrops rather than paint. Others would come in the morning to begin sorting through collections, hauling pieces away.

A nymph down by the foyer had poked through everything at the front desk she had no business touching and found three separate shipping receipts made out to three separate moving companies.

Bea skirted past a stag, exchanging a hurried nod, and then passed a blurry pack of hunting dogs who'd become close friends with the creature they were meant to chase. Women in enormous dresses crowded the stairway, attempting and failing to keep their heaps of silk out of the way. Two girls with more manageable skirts had pressed themselves into a corner of the landing, lips brushing, clutching each other close. Children raced past, and gentlemen tipped their hats to her, and something small and quick and winged darted by overhead.

Everyone, everywhere, a multitude of color. Drips and drabs of paint puddled beneath them, staining Bea's bare feet into a rainbow as she splashed forward. They were friends, all of them, even if the noise and bustle frightened her sometimes. Made her paint feel like it'd dried too tight, a coating she ached to scratch from her limbs. Still, even as she left the crowd behind, she felt at home.

It would all be gone by morning. *They* would all be gone by morning. Watercolor glimmered over her vision, threatening to spill over. She fought to compose herself with a shake of her head.

Bea had lived well past any human lifetime, and still she hated the sting of change. Even a portrait could feel loss, if it hung around long enough. Her sisters liked to say she'd been painted too young to think such heavy thoughts. They'd braid her hair and tip up her chin and wonder if it wouldn't be easier if art couldn't hold so much emotion.

She passed one door, then two, and then stopped before a set twice as tall as her. The handles were brass, well-smoothed by living hands. Ivory dripped and pooled between her toes as she hesitated. The flooring held no temperature, not for her, but her graphite lines felt warm, flushed with nerves and anticipation. Sorrow, flickering at the back of her mind, had no place here. Not yet.

Pulling her hands through her hair, Bea temporarily stained her fingertips brunette. She shook away the misplaced shading. Sometimes, the ladies on the stairway did up her hair, or swapped clothing with her to swath her in their enormous silks. They sketched themselves into something different for a night. Bea had wanted to come as she'd appeared when they'd first met. Hair long and loose, gown plain, gaze pinched and distraught. She came as she'd been painted. Inhaling, she adjusted the sleeves of her dress, and then opened the door.

The ballroom was dark, enormous where the shadows failed to give it any edges. A shiver raced up her back; paint tapped an unsteady beat around her, a mimicry of a rain shower. Nerves chilled the paint smeared across her; she felt the bite of it, the crackle of solidity.

Overhead, a glass dome spread wide, allowing Bea a glimpse of the moon—one of the only friends who'd faultlessly stuck by her throughout her existence. The ballroom was shaded in white and grey and black. Sconces stood empty on the edges of the room; she left off the electric lights they'd installed a few decades back. She could already see him.

"Bea?" His was voice a wonderful, rumbling thing, carved from a mountain, molded with care. There was no need for him to sound so uncertain; the others had made their visits to the ballroom over the past weeks, after one of the early Renaissance boys had spotted the closing notices by the entrance.

Henry said her name as if he'd searched for an excuse to have it pass between his lips.

She never cried; her paint only fell faster, a steady drizzle splattered and absorbed and splattered again. Tucking her arm against her ribs, Bea dug her fingers into the loose fabric by her waist.

"Bea, dear," and he was right there, or trying to be, because stone moved so slowly. Statues held such stiff permanence, none of the impulse portraits allowed. "Please."

He stretched out his arm and, of course, she went to him.

"I'll pull myself together momentarily," she promised, sliding her hand into his bone white grip. He'd lost his color over the centuries, becoming blank in a way her canvas couldn't manage.

He looked exasperated, all pointed stare and shifting lips. If marble could wrinkle, Bea knew she'd have done him in long ago. Henry always reacted the same, whenever she pretended against feeling some emotion. Reaching up, she pressed her thumb between his eyebrows, to stone chiseled perfect and beautiful like all the rest of him. He was young like her; the placard left behind in the shadows detailed some information about his creator and the teenage human he'd been modeled after. Nothing about Henry felt like a copy; the statue had a stubborn will that belonged wholly to him.

Her touch left a fingerprint of paint behind. The smudge soon disappeared, vanished without a thought for how it felt, knowing she could leave no permanent mark behind.

"Henry, be careful," Bea protested when he shifted and nearly fell, trying to wipe away the excess watercolor surely doing unfortunate things to the lines of her face.

"Taking care is useless, now. Don't you think?" Henry asked.

Statues could topple so easily. Several in the atrium had lost pieces of themselves, scattered somewhere in the past after they'd broken. A nose, a limb, crumbs of stone left behind. That was why Henry had been abandoned in the ballroom, out of reach for most guests. In some ways, it was a good thing; he liked the quiet as much as Bea. He held a steadiness about him that calmed her even when the museum seemed too small and loud and crowded.

"No!" Bea surprised herself, the both of them, with the volume of her protest. It echoed as if the walls, the old home, the moon itself agreed with her. "No, Henry. In the morning, when they come for us, they expect you to be as you are now. They'll wrap you up and take you to another museum, and maybe set you up in a corner somewhere. Then, no matter where I end up, I can think of you out there. Safe. You need to be safe."

Art only lasted as long as it was appreciated, and she knew Henry would be magnificent in any form; it was only humanity she needed to worry about if he started to lose pieces of himself. They might not handle him so carefully anymore, or give him the good placement he deserved. Paintings didn't need to hold themselves so carefully; Bea didn't have much to fear when walking at night, besides avoiding stepping outdoors during a rainstorm. By day, there was every chance Bea's portrait would be shoved away into a storage room, or that she'd be lost or damaged in transit. Every chance she wouldn't have a home as nice as this to pace through on quiet, empty nights. It would be fine, even if she was afraid, so long as *Henry* was fine.

"It would be much easier to mind your advice if you would be there to help me remember," Henry said.

She scoffed, an ugly, angry sound. The best kind, that tended to conceal heartbreak. Bea prodded his chest with another huff, until carefully sculpted muscle pressed close to her.

"You should have considered that before you did—you did *this*," Bea said, gesturing between them.

Henry gave her that look again, the one that said she fooled no one.

"Fell in love with you?" he asked, a solid hand resting at the back of her neck for a moment before he pulled her closer. "How many times must I apologize for that?"

"Always." Her voice muffled as she pressed her face against his chest. Solid and cool and silent, and certainly not smeared with paint because she was certainly not crying.

It was a terrible thing to love someone from another collection. Art was a beautiful contradiction, both eternal and impermanent. Exhibits and tastes changed; funding was lost or gained. Nothing guaranteed that she and Henry would be housed in the same new location.

They'd met shortly after her painting had arrived, a few decades back. Her sisters had gone off to explore, and the halls had been so busy, bright against the night's darkness. Too many portraits and busts and sculptures; absolutely no room to breathe. Bea had found the ballroom, which exuded the calm she'd craved. In her old home, she'd taken to hiding in the attic. She'd loved this new, quiet place. Henry, she hadn't expected.

Henry, who couldn't move very far or very fast because of what he was, what he was made of, so he could not roam through the museum. He'd been amused by her fluster because of the way she'd barged in, and presumably because of his appearance. Cloth draped in precariously carved folds around his waist. When Bea had eventually admitted her embarrassment came from his catching her panicking, and she had no interest in finding a shadowed corner like many of her sisters liked to do with their suitors, he'd only seemed relieved. Shrugged, when Bea told Henry she didn't think much of kissing anyone. His stone still felt warm and safe, when he held her close to calm her ragged breathing, and that was that for them. Bea had returned to the ballroom again, and again, and again.

They'd spent nights whispering stories of past collections and old homes. The studio where Henry had first opened his eyes; the countryside where Bea had opened hers. Until, eventually, this statue had claimed what heart a portrait could have.

Bea loved him so much it hurt. Little knives of loss already chipped away at her inside. She'd never much minded the idea of leaving a place; home wasn't a location for her.

"Stop thinking so hard," Henry demanded, wrapping her hair around his fingertips. "I swear your worries should cause your paint to bubble."

Bea pouted, knowing he would see through the expression and it would make him smile. Then his breath caught, gaze slipping past her.

"Do you hear that, dear?"

Music stirred elsewhere in the museum, jostling within Bea's chest until her watercolors felt heavy. At this distance, it was impossible to say who'd pulled their instruments down from their frames. Too many musicians lived in the museum; music was a thing trapped beside the creative process, the perfect accompaniment.

Notes swelled, tentatively at first, until they agreed upon a rhythm.

It was too quiet, but Bea's hands found their familiar place on his shoulders, fingertips pressing against the curve of his neck. His settled near her waist, holding her close and steadying himself whenever they shifted. Swayed, too slowly to really accompany the music. Bea liked it best that way. She tipped her head back, wanting to drink in the sight of him before the drought came.

It was difficult to track a gaze with no iris, no pupil. She knew, brushstrokes running hot, that Henry watched her, too.

"Remember the night we escaped into the garden?" Henry asked, lips softening with the memory.

"I remember you nearly chipped yourself on the doorframe."

"That wasn't my fault, Bea. You unbalance me."

She wrinkled her nose, feigning displeasure. Her grip tightened, lest he slip on the colors gathering beneath their feet.

"There are so many stars out there, Bea," Henry said. "No matter where one goes, the stars are always there to greet you. I find it an easy way to remember I'm not alone."

He *had* spent so many years alone in the ballroom with only the occasional visitor, watching the sky through the domed ceiling. It was easiest for Henry not to stray far from his placement. Even that night in the garden, they hadn't spent long outside. It'd taken some work to get Henry back onto his pedestal.

She'd borrowed a dress from one of her sisters, colors dropping off into the dry grass poking her slick feet. Henry had looked like something built from moonlight. So solid, striping silver and grey. His gaze so soft and lovely that she'd finally believed he truly didn't mind that she thought she'd never want to kiss anyone, that her love was enough on its own. Had always been enough for Henry; it was only Bea that'd taken a while longer to realize this.

"You pointed out the color bleeding through my dress," Bea sighed. That was the problem with borrowing from a different idea; the white from the dress she was meant to wear had tried to come through, splotching blush pink with ivory.

"It'd been so long since I'd spoken to anyone more than once. Let alone someone like you," Henry smiled.

He'd looked sick that night, if a statue could be sick, and had wrung her hand ragged. Crickets sung an irregular harmony around them, and the hillside spilled downward into a gorgeous sprawl of humanity's electric lights, and all the while he'd looked at Bea like she was the sun itself.

"Tell me again?" Bea asked. "What you said afterward?"

His chin dipped and her gaze nearly did, too, before she remembered she needed to memorize this. Them.

"I told you that I love you, Bea, dear." Henry's voice rumbled, a thinly contained quake. "I do, still. I love you, here. I'll love you through what comes next."

She smeared watercolor over his collarbone when she leaned in close. Henry had never minded her smothering an emotion or two against him.

This unraveled her, pulled harder than the decades, the dust, the unchecked fingerprints. They would move on and live on and no one would know what they'd lost. The guests who came by daylight would never see that one decision, one failure, had destroyed her more thoroughly than any corrosion could.

"Do you wish it had gone differently? The night we met?" Bea asked, sniffing, ignoring the colors fading across his stone.

"Of course," Henry said. "I would do away with you shrieking when you first spotted me moving."

Snorting, undignified, Bea shrugged helplessly. "I'd never seen anything like you before."

There'd been no statues in her old home. Henry, half-crouched, all in shadow, had startled her more than the overcrowded hallways. She'd cried a little afterward from embarrassment, while trying to apologize for screaming in his face. It'd only added to her panicked fluster. She'd hoped he hadn't noticed—sometimes all the dripping paint made it hard to tell, but Henry could always figure her out in the end. He'd held her hand, having her focus on his calm, steady stone.

"I wish we'd been painted together," Bea said, grip tightening. "I don't regret a moment of it, but I wish that it mattered. How much I love you."

Henry said nothing, but his hands were so gentle on her and his breath stuttered with a devastating catch. The music swelled, carrying and cradling them together for just one night more.

Fingers, featherlight and strong as a hillside, pulled through her hair. The moon had slipped away from their dome, reluctantly taking her light away and letting in the dawn.

"It's time," Henry said.

Time. They had so much of it, as long as they were deemed worthy of preservation. If not for the changes in the guests who came—shifting fashions and wrinkling faces—time would have paused for them. There was no need to worry over the future when one was happy. Bea wanted an impossible forever. Change made her want to cling to her sisters, to have them reassure her everything would turn out alright for them in the end.

Bea helped Henry to his pedestal. His movements were stiff but sure; her hands slipped over him, memorizing his weight against her palms as he leaned against her for support. Then he was stable, drawing himself upright and nearly out of her reach.

She had a frame to return to.

"Bea." His frown made her think she might admit to crying, this once.

She caught his hand within hers, keeping them in this moment.

"I wish to say something horrifically romantic, but the words escape me," Bea said, pressing her lips together to smother a rueful smile.

Henry lifted her hand, kissing her knuckles as if they were made of something more precious than old paint.

"Allow me, then," he said. "Remember me whenever you see the stars. My love for you burns brighter than them, but they'll be a nice placeholder, for now."

Bea's smile escaped her then, dangerously watery. "That'll do, Henry. I love you, too."

She left him standing there, his gaze a tether at the back of her neck. Gathering her skirt in her hands, she clutched the gauzy material so she wouldn't be tempted to go back and fill her hands with his instead.

The halls were quieter upon her return. Children and animals sat snug in their canvases. There were other frantic, whispered goodbyes that Bea ignored as she passed; privacy was the only gift she could afford to give.

This was the end and the beginning.

Bea said goodbye to marbled halls and the grand, sweeping stairway. To galleries and arched window frames and a half-forgotten ballroom left behind. Her sisters, the rest of her collection, already sat tucked within their canvases. Charles was there too, his red and yellow and orange calm, sleeping. Bea gathered her skirts by her knees so she wouldn't trip, climbing into her frame.

There was a chance this was goodbye not just to the museum, but to everything. If no one wanted to display Bea any longer. If she went missing or her frame ended up damaged, lost. It frustrated her, to have the chance to outlive any human several times over, and simultaneously have no control over her own future.

Henry would think of her always, out there somewhere, wandering a new location. Searching for a new quiet place where she could tip her head back and see the stars. Even if the worst happened, she would remain preserved in a statue's fond memories.

Bea closed her eyes.

KAYLA WHITTLE works in marketing and social media for a medical publisher. She has previously had a short story published in Luna Station Quarterly. *Most often she can be found on Instagram @caughtbetweenthepages or on Twitter @kaylawhitwrites. When not writing, she's usually busy reading, embroidering, or planning her next Disney vacation. She currently resides in New Jersey.*

THE SINGING

Georgia Cook

Mist churned beneath the horses' hooves, billowing out behind the carriage like a great white cape. Colette stared from the windows at the passing forest, trying to imagine a world beyond the whiteness; a world still bright with sunlight, where conversations were loud and joyous, not reduced to mournful whispers.

It was impossible, here, to imagine such a world.

The mists curled away as the carriage left the forest, marking the slow descent down a winding track into a low valley. The landscape here dropped away sharply, rising up into steep mountains on either side. In the centre of this strange natural bowl, harsh against the land-scape and green fields and lush trees, sat Belleview house.

With its towering grey walls and glinting black windows, Belleview stood in stark contrast to its name. It put Colette in mind of a huge rotten tooth, squatting in the open mouth of the valley. Save for the Groundskeeper's hut and the vast lake behind the house, it was the only landmark for miles.

How Richard could stand to live here, Colette would never know.

Turning down towards the house, the carriage passed a natural bump in the valley. Too small to be a hill, too sharp to be incidental, it rose long and green on the hill overlooking the house. Colette watched it pass, remembering the day she and Richard had trekked up the hill to see it.

"The Belleview Mound," he'd called it, motioning with a grand sweep of his arm. "*Mound of The Beauty.*"

" . . . What is it?" she'd asked, and hated herself for asking such a simple question.

Richard shrugged. "Some ancient lord, buried on the land. The locals will tell you all sorts of rubbish about banshees and spirits. Utter rot, of course."

"Banshees?"

Richard grinned. "Didn't you know, Colly? You're marrying into a family with a pet Beast! *The Belleview Banshee.* Lock your windows if you hear wailing across the hills tonight, she'll be foretelling a gruesome death!"

"And does she?" Colette didn't like it when Richard called her Colly.

" . . . Does she what?"

"*Wail?*"

Richard snorted. "Well, if she exists at all she's awfully shy. I've not heard a *peep.*" He reached out, his fingers brushing Colette's arm. "Don't be scared, Colly. It's just local superstition."

"I'm not scared." she'd said, pulling her arm away.

The topic had turned to wedding plans and Richard's job in London, Belleview Mound and its Banshee forgotten, but for weeks after that Colette had suffered terrible dreams of women lying beneath the earth at Belleview, their eyes closed, their lips blue from cold, their hair fanning out around them like strange, tangled roots.

She wondered what it must be like down in the deepest dark; what urge could pull someone from the earth to wail for the death of a total stranger.

What terrible longing.

Richard was waiting to greet Colette on the long gravel drive in front of the house.

He helped her down from the carriage, wearing one of his wide not-quite smiles, kissed her cheek, and asked one of the maids to escort her upstairs, making promises to meet Colette at dinner.

And just like that, Colette was already alone.

Richard's parents, in a rare display of modern thinking, had taken themselves off to Edinburgh for the week, allowing the young couple time alone together at Belleview—or alone as one could be with twelve assorted servants.

Colette had been allowed a room to herself up near the attic—because modern thinking was modern thinking, but sharing a room with one's fiancé was a step too far. It was spacious enough, with rich red wallpaper and a rolling view of the lake. A fire had been laid in the grate, and the sheets on the large four poster bed were freshly changed.

Colette's travelling case was waiting for her on the bed. Colette shot a glance over her shoulder, before kneeling down and throwing open the lid, pawing through the skirts and shoes and dresses until her fingers brushed the little envelope concealed at the bottom. Her heart gave a jolt. Carefully, carefully, she eased it out.

The paper still smelt of Amelia, still crinkled from Amelia's touch. Colette's chest ached to read the familiar spidery handwriting:

My Darling.

Colette could still feel the brush of Amelia's hair, the teasing warmth of her fingertips. Better than a whispered love song, better than a stolen kiss in the midnight shadows.

She'd worn a dress of forest green velvet to see Colette off that morning. Colette's heart had lept to see her there, standing amidst the luggage and carrying cases piled on her father's driveway. She'd hoped Amelia would clasp her arm, scream and shout, demand Colette reconsider her unwanted betrothal. Perhaps they would flee; run away to Paris or Spain, start a life entirely of their own. Instead, Amelia had pressed the envelope hurriedly into Colette's hand as she helped her into the carriage.

"For luck," she'd whispered. "For when you arrive."

"I'll write to you," Colette promised. "I'll write every day. You'll be sick of me!"

Amelia smiled a sad, soft little smile. "Of course."

Of course.

Colette had watched from the back window as the carriage pulled away down the drive, until Amelia was nothing more than a vague silhouette on the horizon, her red curls tumbling around her shoulders, her dress of forest green velvet swirling in the wind.

That night Colette lay awake in the unfamiliar bed, watching shadows cluster across the ceiling. It was too quiet in the countryside; Colette listened for the rutted *clump-clump* of cartwheels, the shouts and distant conversations of night-time London, but all she heard was the rustle of wind through the trees, the far-off rush of water—

. . . and the singing.

Colette froze.

It was a woman's voice, soft and sweet, echoing from somewhere out across the hills. Colette couldn't make out the words, but the tune tugged at her chest, wrapping a hand of strange sorrow around her heart. Was it a maid singing a lullaby somewhere in the house? A snatch of birdsong out in the woods? No ... no ...

It was coming from further than that; out towards the lake.

Colette lay rigid in the darkness, listening, until at last the song faded and the night was once again still.

Colette asked Richard about the singing over breakfast—a sterile affair of toast and tea in Belleview's impressive dining room.

"Perhaps you heard the banshee, Colly," he said, grinning across the table.

"But it wasn't screaming," Colette insisted. "It was *singing*."

Richard stabbed at his toast with a butterknife. "I'll have the game-keeper search the ground if it worries you. Keep an eye out for tres-passers."

"I'm not worried," said Colette, automatically, but she knew Rich-ard wouldn't understand. She wanted to explain that the singing hadn't felt threatening; it had been beautiful. So, so beautiful. She wanted to say that for the first time in days, the first time in weeks, she'd felt the same wondrous ache as when she lay in Amelia's arms.

She longed to hear it again.

Colette lay awake in the darkness for two more nights, but the song didn't return.

During the day she wandered the halls of Belleview manor, lost and overwhelmed, dwarfed by generations of antique finery, wonder-ing how anyone could live in a place so quiet. In the evenings she wrote out her heart on sheets and sheets of letter paper, splattering ink across her freckled forearms.

No letters arrived from home, no mail of any kind, and in the si-lence Colette couldn't help but feel she'd crossed into a new world; an isolated bauble encased in woodlands and rising fields.

She wondered what the singer had been doing, all alone in the dark.

She wondered if she might have dreamt it after all.

She wondered if Amelia would write.

*

A week went by without change. Colette resigned herself once more to aching silence. Perhaps the countryside had disturbed her. Perhaps the impending wedding was conjuring strange dreams . . .

—she jolted awake, blinking in the sudden darkness, her heart pounding. Slowly, shapes of her Belleview bedroom merged out of the shadows. The fire burned low in the fireplace. The air was still with a prickling coldness.

. . . and the softest of whispers wound through the curtains.

Colette jerked upright, scrabbled in the darkness for her shawl, and rushed to the window. The grounds of Belleview house lay dark and empty below her. She could hear the singing now, this close to the window, but the words were still too soft to discern. Colette deliberated a moment, then lit the candle on her bedside table, grasped her shawl tightly, and crept out into the corridor.

No sounds from above or below. No floorboard creaks. Only the distant singing followed Colette down the stairs in the darkness, across the hall—careful not to wake Mr Garris the butler, asleep in his room by the kitchen—through the front door, and out into the night.

The world shone silver and black in the moonlight. The hills loomed high overhead, sharp as distant teeth. Out here, the singing filled the midnight world, seeping into every crack and corner, sweeping along the grass, always just a touch too soft to understand. Colette followed it across the lawn, mist curling around her ankles, dew stinging her feet.

Up ahead lay Belleview lake; a glimmering black void lit by a high white moon. Colette froze, her breath misting in the air. Crouched on the shoreline, the pitch black water swirling about her ankles, stood the silhouette of a woman. She was bent over the water, scrubbing furiously at something hidden beneath the surface. As she scrubbed she sang; an outpouring of grief so raw that it hurt Colette's chest.

"*Excuse me!*" Colette whispered, surprised at her own voice.

Excuse me, who are you? Why are you singing? Why does it sound like every pain this place has caused me—

The woman turned sharply. Colette caught a glimpse of pale flesh and bruise-blue lips. The song continued unchanged, emanating from a mouth hanging open in wordless supplication. This close, it seemed to twist the world, warping the trees and sending the moon spiralling in a flash of silver. It filled Colette's head, bearing down her lungs, grasping her chest.

The woman lifted her arms from the lake, finally revealing a bundle of sodden velvet, thick with water. Velvet dyed a deep forest green.

Colette awoke to Richard kneeling at her bedside, clutching her hand. Sunlight streamed through the curtains behind him, illuminating the dark red wallpaper and gleaming brass fittings of Colette's bedroom. No moonlight, no pitch black lake, no singing.

" . . . What were you doing on the mound?" Richard whispered. "What were you *doing*, Colette?"

" . . . On the mound?" Colette mumbled, turning her head.

"The servants found you on the Mound last night. You could have frozen to death." Richard leaned in close, wearing an expression of unfamiliar concern. "Were you sleepwalking, Colly?"

Colette struggled to focus on Richard's lips. The world was soft and pliable, slipping through her fingers like warm water. Dust hung in the air, twisting through the shafts of morning sunlight, as insubstantial as a dream. For the first time in weeks, Colette felt at peace.

"Yes ... " she whispered, as Richard's face twisted and stretched before her eyes. "Yes ... I think I was ... "

Colette remained in bed for three days, delirious with fever, humming strings of disjointed notes, her hands working back and forth across the bedspread. She slept fitfully, waking only to accept sips of water, and to ask if any letters had arrived. In her dreams it was always midnight, always still. The lake shone silver behind her, lighting the way as Colette climbed Belleview mound.

The earth was cold and pliable beneath her feet, shifting beneath her weight. Up ahead, the mound lay open to the stars. Colette reached the top and lay down on the loamy earth, breathing the scent of mud and wild flowers. She listened for the humming, for the stir of female forms deep beneath the earth. And when at last she heard their voices, heard the muffled scratching of searching hands ...

She lifted her voice and sang.

At last the fever broke, and Colette was allowed to leave her room. She walked the corridors of Belleview in a daze, barely speaking, her eyes listless and tired. The servants whispered amongst themselves, gossiping about the poor city girl, unable to cope. Would Master Richard postpone the wedding? Would he cancel the marriage altogether? Everyone knew the union was purely political. What would people *say*?

Colette heard the whispers, but said nothing. Each night she sat at her window, staring out across the grounds. Each night she waited for the woman to sing again; for the mound on the hill to split open at last, so she could raise her voice as she had in her dreams.

But the song never came. The night remained silent, the mound on the hill empty and unchanged.

When at last a letter arrived from home, edged in gold and printed on expensive white paper, Colette wasn't surprised to receive it. It was a wedding invitation, inviting Colette to *The Joyful Union of Amelia Baker and Charles King*. Below it, in spidery handwriting as familiar as Colette's own, was a single phrase:

Perhaps This Is Better.

Colette sat on the library floor, the song pounding through her skull, tracing each word over and over with a finger, and at last understood:

The Banshee sang to foretell a death, but there was more than one kind of dying.

Belleview house was hers, the forests and lawns were hers. The mound was hers, high on its lonely hill. Even Richard, stiff and awkward and unyielding, was hers. And maybe one day a child would be hers as well, to raise in glorious isolation.

But Amelia would never be hers, just as she would never be Amelia's.

That was the loss. That was grief, risen from the earth to commiserate with the cold, unfeeling sky.

Perhaps This Is Better.

That night Colette slipped from her bedchamber, out into the garden, and up, up to Belleview mound. She felt her way blindly, her fingers biting into the soft earth, her bare toes slipping and sliding as she climbed. The moon hung behind her, bulbous and full, watching.

At last Colette reached the top of the mound. She clambered to her feet, unsteady in her sodden nightdress, and turned. Belleview lay beneath her, its walls high and forbidding, its windows dark. Down there, somewhere, Richard lay sleeping. Colette's future hung quietly in wardrobes and antique drawers, in the marriage bed she would one day occupy, waiting for her to inhabit it.

Colette lifted her face to the sky, breathing in the loamy air, watching the curtain of stars, then she opened her mouth and sang. She sang for her loss, she sang for her isolation, she sang for a title she had never truly wanted, and a husband who would never be hers. She sang from the deepest pit of her broken heart. She sang out to all those consumed by sorrow; who understood the aching wordlessness of grief.

In the darkness they heard, and in the darkness they came.

Across the fields they glided. Across the lake, through the trees, their grey cloaks billowing out behind them, carrying the fog and mist. They opened their arms to Colette, calling back through the darkness, their mouths wide in supplication.

Not screaming, not screaming at all.

Colette watched their approach.

How was a banshee made? She wondered. How was a Banshee formed? The urge to sink oneself into the deep dark lake, to drown in mud and wretchedness, to howl at the world for a sorrow you didn't own.

The cold caught in Colette's throat, sharp enough to hurt. "Take me," she whispered, holding out her hands. "Take me, please."

She was the mistress of Belleview; she would sing for those who had come before her, and she would sing for those who came next. Every little death. Every little unbecoming. Every shattering of a tiny world.

Oh, how she would sing.

GEORGIA COOK is an illustrator and writer from London. She is the winner of the LISP 2020 Flash Fiction Prize, and has been shortlisted for the Bridport Prize and Reflex Fiction Award, among others. She has also written for numerous podcasts, webcomics and anthologies. She can be found on twitter at @georgiacooked and on her website at https://www.georgiacookwriter.com/.

HER FIRST FULL BREATH

Emmie Christie

The men filled their lungs for several minutes before they leapt off the pier, one at a time, the weights on their feet pulling them down.

Before they jumped, their bodies rippled with the sweetness of the air, lightening them so they bounced a little off the ground. They had a certain elation in the sway of their shoulders, and Cam practiced it too, switching her weight from one foot to another, and sucking in the wind as it passed. The air across the world had a tinge of honey, but here in Faize, it sweetened further in the swirling thunderstorms contained by the surrounding mountains, and changed those who breathed it.

Varin strode up, next in line. His already large chest inflated to twice its normal size, his sweet red lips curving high. He bounced a little. She waved to him, and he waved back before he jumped, the weights towing his near-weightless body down into the sea.

Her ribs refused to elongate further, and Cam coughed from the sudden stop.

"There you are," a voice said from behind her. She whirled. Her mother waited, ramrod straight, as if hung on a coatrack. "I told you to stop watching the men. They'll be back before too long, and we must sell the pearls in the valley."

Cam swallowed her groan and kept her thoughts small. Arguing with her mother produced no profit either way, and Faize had taught her that life ran on profit.

"Yes, mother." She traipsed along down the path. Her mother minced her steps like she did green onions, small and quick and determined. Her waist, trained the smallest in Faize to the width of an arm, showed the beating of her heart through her spine, and the rise and fall of her lungs, stacked atop each other. Next to her, Cam might as well have been an ogre, with her waist as large as a man's thigh.

They reached the village. The women bustled around, packs of pearls on their backs. The dawn had ripened into late morning. Cam dashed to gather her share of pearls, most of them fist-sized, stuffing them into a backpack. Her mother frowned.

"These are getting smaller. The men need to stay longer than four hours, I say. Back in my day, they'd stay down for eight."

Her uncle, one of the few men in the village who could not dive due to weak lungs, snorted. "Elaine, you'd ask the mountains themselves to flatten if you could."

Leaving the mountain felt like leaving paradise. The air staled and flattened compared to the honey-sweetness of Faize, and the caravan of women trailed down into the valley where the market bustled. Cam always wavered on her feet, and her vision whitened for a few seconds until she stabilized her breath.

Everywhere else in the world craved Faize pearls, as the only place in the world where they originated, so they never had trouble selling them. But some people complained about the smaller pearls as of late and paid less for them. Her mother's gracious, put-on smile twitched when someone tried to bargain with her. "One hundred gold? My dear, we must clothe our children and feed our men, what do you think we can do with that? We sell these for one fifty, no less."

"But there's someone else who sells a much larger pearl. Once a year."

Elaine's jaw tightened. The mysterious pearl seller had surfaced in conversation a few times in the past years, and it had cut into their profits more each time. "Well, feel free to buy that pearl then."

The buyer hemmed and hawed but ended up purchasing the pearls. Cam watched her mother. She watched people a lot, afraid that should she say something, her breath would give out in the middle of her sentence. She puffed just walking up and down the trail to the valley market.

Her mother shone as the jewel of Faize, displaying her figure with the unbending nature of her posture. She'd run the council for ten years now and kept the people of the village fed well with her skills at netting profits. The women of the valley all emulated her as they wandered past, straightening themselves, sucking in their waists. Cam had the opposite urge. She missed the sweetness of the mountain air, of filling her lungs with its honey so full. *What is wrong with me?*

"Don't let the Shark see you doing that," her uncle said, nodding to her mother. His chest rose and fell with short breaths like a woman.

237

"I know, I know," Cam said. "But I can't help it." The words poured out of her. "I want to breathe more, not less. I want to hold it longer. I want to—" She cut herself off in the middle, biting her tongue. She couldn't say that.

Her uncle raised his eyebrows. He paused, then leaned closer. "You know . . . there's a doctor, deep in the sea. It's said she can enlarge someone's lungs." He shrugged. "Of course, you didn't hear that from me."

Cam's jaw dropped. "You mean, anyone? Even me?"

Her uncle leaned back, his eyes flicking to the front of the vendor stall. Elaine, Cam's mother, strode back.

"Are you both just sitting here? Sell your pearls, girl, by the mountain, or I'll put you back in your waist trainer, see I won't."

"Yes, mother," Cam said, but her heart pounded like a large drum in her chest.

Cam trained with the men the next morning, inhaling deep lungfuls of air. Her body seemed lighter. Out on the pier, even the possibility of incubating that air in the deep sea expanded her chest more than ever. Her legs twitched, wanting to jump, but she kept filling her lungs as much as she could. The dizziness that had always accompanied her had lessened as of late. The longer she held the air, the stronger she became.

The men shot sideways glances at her, of course. "I won't jump," she assured them, the lie sweet in her throat. *Not yet anyway.* She'd always loomed above the other girls her age, and now she used it to her advantage, not backing down from their daunting height or questioning looks.

Varin smiled at her. He sidled up to her, his large strides eating the distance between them much too fast for her heart to handle. She grinned up at him. "Escaping the Shark?" he asked, and she giggled, unable to speak while holding her breath like the men could.

His proximity made her want to twirl in a dress, to flutter her fingers, to stand up straight like her mother did to show off her figure. He didn't seem to care that she flouted council rules. Her mother, the Shark's, rules.

"Wish me luck," Varin said, and jumped. She watched him until the darker waters swallowed his silhouette.

How far down did the doctor live? Deeper than the men submerged every day. Deep in the heart of the water, where the men said the pressure squeezed too much. *This is crazy.* The thought ricocheted off the inside of her ribs and turned inside out. *No crazier than a woman wanting to get bigger just to breathe more. No, I'm doing this.*

That evening, Varin handed her the two pearls he had incubated. Round and heavy as duck eggs, they shimmered in the evening light.

"Get a good price for mine?"

The question hung between them. The custom of such a question shone in Varin's eyes—he wanted her to go steady with him. She'd liked Varin since she'd grown breasts, since she'd seen him dive the first time. He parted the water with grace and power. She hadn't known if he liked her, though, with her wide shoulders and waist. She hadn't worn the corset trainer enough as a child, not like her mother had wanted her to. Cam liked the dimple in his chin. She reached for it, now, and he took her hand and laid it on his cheek.

"I'll make sure of it," she said. "See you tomorrow."

The men stayed submerged in the sea from three to six hours at a time. The longer they could hold the sweet air of Faize, the more that the sea compressed the air, rounding it into pearls in their lungs, larger and larger until they could hold their breath no more.

She trained with the men early every day. They didn't seem to care, not as much as her mother would have if she had known.

"How do you know how far down to go?" Cam asked. She had worked on speaking while holding her breath. Her body had lightened so much it almost bounced.

Varin shifted next to her. "There's a marker down there. At two hundred feet, we stop."

"How do you go so far down, and for so long? Four hours of holding your breath!"

"It's not how far down you go," Varin said. He grinned as she bobbed around. "It's how much you concentrate. It's fun, though, isn't it?"

"Yes!"

That morning, she waited after each of the men had jumped, after Varin had said, "Wish me luck," once more, and she fitted one small weight on to her buoyant body, and splashed in. She did not start well, as she'd never done it before, and jumbled her limbs and rolled around, until the small weight took hold of her and tugged her down twenty feet or so.

The sea did not pressure her lungs at this depth, so near the surface, so the air inside her did not compress. How deep down did the doctor live? she wondered again. She wanted to ask her uncle for further details, but he had stayed away the past few weeks, perhaps avoiding Elaine. Well, she'd just have to find out herself. She paddled around in the light surface water, working her arms and practicing holding her breath. Her lungs burned, and she ached to suck in more air, but she held it.

After a week of this, she wore heavier weights that pulled her fifty feet down, and the compression started in her lungs. The pressure added to the bubble of air she held, pushing on all sides. She gritted her teeth, and her ribcage protested, but after practice she could submerge eighty feet. Faize's sweet air hardened into a glaze, the smallest of candies inside her lungs.

Am I growing a pearl?

No, that was crazy! Only men had the capacity for that!

She watched for the men in the sea, but they still floated much further down. Varin, however, did look at her now in the mornings with a thoughtful confusion, and one day he asked, "Don't you want to stay on the land more?"

She responded with effort. "I like it . . . here." She'd almost said she liked it in the sea, where the air compressed inside her. What if she could grow pearls, too? The last time, it had seemed like the density of her breath had hardened into a solid thing. An impossible thing.

241

"You know, I bring up pretty big pearls," he said. "You don't have to . . ." he paused, his red lips curving down. "Encourage me."

Her eyes widened and she coughed, losing her breath. "Oh, I know you do!" Cam said. "I'm out here for me."

His gaze darkened. He lowered his head, and then dove straight into the sea before he had filled his lungs for very long at all. She watched where he had gone down for a long time.

He thought I came out here to encourage him to do better? He thinks what he brings in isn't large enough? She cursed her mother's influence and constant complaining. *I am not her,* she whispered to herself, and started to hold her breath again.

The doubt began when the pearls did grow inside her. She brought forth the first two, small as grains of sand, after the first time she stayed in the sea longer than half an hour. Perfectly round and smooth, compressed by the pressure at one hundred feet, they'd sell for less than five gold. But she had done it. Something that women didn't hold the capacity for. And the experience—she felt bad for the other women who'd never tasted forming one. She even felt bad for those in the market who bought the pearls just for their rarity. Once taken out of the body, they had no taste, of course, not like it did while forming them.

She pocketed them. She couldn't pass them off as from any of the men, or her mother would start no end of a riot. Who would dare bring back such small pearls? Her mother the Shark would hunt down the truth for sure, and with the power of the council behind her, Cam shivered at what she might do.

But she could not back down now, not when she could grow pearls! Her ribs had even expanded a bit on their own to accommodate the gems inside, and her limbs had thickened, too, with muscle, from her swimming every day.

"There's no help for it," her mother announced one day, while they tramped down into the valley for market. "You must go back to waist training. I'll fit you with a corset myself."

Cam bit back a retort. She'd trained her waist since childhood and had never taken to it as well as the other girls in the village. Every girl hated it, of course, forcing the indents of their middles to sharpen, but she'd *hated* it. Could she even stomach it at all, now?

She couldn't. When her mother cinched the corset trainer around her, Cam blacked out from the lack of breath.

She woke up in the sick room, her mother's anxious face hovering over her. "Dear, something is wrong." She paced in her ramrod straight way, without the bend and sway of hips. But she did not release Cam out of the corset, and Cam drifted like she did in the sea, like she was air being compressed, her body a pearl to be sold.

In the distance, her uncle's voice sounded: "It's killing her, Elaine. You have to take the inner corset off."

"Nonsense," her mother's voice said. "Something is wrong with her! She's gotten taller. Broad shouldered, like—like a man."

Her uncle sighed, and their voices floated away on the waves of consciousness. Her body rebelled, her lungs burning, and she woke up in the sick room to Varin and Elaine's faces, and in desperation for just one full breath, she inhaled the way she wanted, without stopping, filling her lungs like she did on the pier—even with her mother there watching.

The corset trainer split. She gasped and coughed for what felt like years, with them looking on in horror. Well, did Varin look at her like that? She couldn't tell through the haze. She stumbled to her feet.

Her mother stepped towards her, but Cam held her hands out. "What—" she gasped for breath. "Did uncle Quinn mean, when he said, 'inner corset'?"

Her mother's frown deepened. "Dear. You must lay back down. You are exhibiting—"

"What. Did. He. Mean?"

When her mother didn't answer, Cam shouted, "What did you do to me?!"

"The same as every other girl in Faize!"

Her mother had raised her voice for the first time since Cam could remember. The woman's tiny chest heaved, and her bloodshot eyes bulged. She'd been crying. Varin looked back and forth between the two women, and his broad shoulders curved in on themselves in confusion.

"Every infant girl," her mother said, in her customary lower, controlled tone, "is fitted with a metal corset. We open the chest and place it before the bones can harden. It's the best time for it, you see, so the organs grow right."

Cam blinked at her mother. "Grow . . . . right."

She had a corset inside her, around her own ribcage, constraining her breath.

"Only yours didn't! Your lungs refused to go vertical, like the other girls." Her mother pursed her lips. "Probably because you shirked your waist training."

Roaring sounded in Cam's ears. "I wasn't born like this?" Her breath shortened, and dizziness returned, her old friend. "You mean, without this corset, my lungs would be larger?"

"Of course," Her mother said. "But I'm thinking we should do reduction surgery on you, now that nothing else has worked." Cam ran out. She could not stay there any longer. *It's not my fault.* The thought echoed all around her.

All her life, she'd longed to just swell her insides but had instead pushed herself to decrease, to shrink, to minimize, and it made her want to tear out her hair. She dashed for the pier, and Varin and her mother hurried after her. Her mother could not keep up, of course, no woman could run as fast as Cam now, not with their lung capacity reduced to half. Varin, though, reached her after a few strides.

"Don't," she growled. "Don't ask me to go back."

His eyes flicked over her, perhaps still in shock.

"Do *you* think I'm ugly?"

His mouth worked in half a breath, and that was all the answer she needed. She pushed him away, and ran, and ran, and he did not chase her. She pulled in all the air she could and dove off the pier.

She swam deep, as far down as she could without weights. She wouldn't play her mother's games of attraction, not anymore. She didn't care about that when she just wanted to breathe, and condense her breath into dense pearls, and why was that such a masculine dream?

She hadn't pulled near enough air while running. It compressed too fast, ready for her to return to the surface, but *she wasn't ready.*

She dove further down, and the compression pushed on her chest. She would not go back, she refused. Would Varin hate her forever, now, knowing that her body had no chance of delicacy? She would never possess the tiny waist her mother had perfected. She still liked to wear dresses, was that wrong, too?

How far down had she gone?

How long had she submerged?

The tiny air-pearl inside her had grown to the size of a thumb. It tasted sweeter. She swam down farther. She held onto the pearl like a lifeline and Varin's words echoed in her mind: "It's not how long you're down there, it's how much you concentrate," and she concentrated, and her body inched down, and down, with each pull of her tiring arms.

I must find the doctor. I must find the doctor.

The pearl grew and grew to fist-sized, pushing out the metal cage that surrounded her ribs, straining them. She passed the marker displaying where the men stopped, at two hundred feet. And still she parted the waters with her fingers, though they trembled.

"You called for me?"

A woman with the face of her mother, but a much, much bigger body, emerged from the shadows of the sea. As large as a house, she had muscles and thickness on her upper thighs, and something about her waist looked right in proportion to her breasts. She had a beauty Cam had never witnessed, a generosity of hip, and in her smile. She looked . . . happy. It was the most gorgeous kind of beauty. *I want that.*

Keeping the pearl of air firm in her lungs, she jerked her head to the woman. She hadn't tried speaking underwater before. The men had said that it was possible if one controlled the breath with precision. "Are you the doctor of the sea? I want to enlarge—" Wait. Her purpose had changed. "I mean, can you take out an inner corset?" The pressure of the sea weighed on her more when she spoke, the effort of not releasing her breath more difficult. Without the momentum, her body wanted to float upwards, and she had no weights to hold herself in place.

The woman sighed. "Elaine is still pushing that on girls, is she? I had hoped she had figured it out by now, after the harm it did to her."

"Are you . . . related?"

She laughed. "My sister. One of us obsessed with attraction, the other with the air. Can you guess which one I am?" She wiggled her hips with the suggestion the size of houses.

"But I've never seen you. No one ever spoke of you. My uncle— he didn't even say who you were."

"My name's Seerah. I've never seen fit to come back around. I only have to come up to breathe once a year, and the pearl I produce . . .

well." She laughed. "Let's just say it's enough to keep Elaine on her toes."

"You're the other supplier!"

"Indeed. You did well to reach down this far, with an inner corset." Seerah frowned. "My dear girl, I am sorry, but I am no doctor. I broke out of my corset by coming down here."

"But I still have it in me. Even here." Cam gritted her teeth. The pressure redoubled inside her at the despairing thought.

"You must go down further, to break it. The pearls snap it free once you get far enough down."

Seerah pointed down.

"I can't—I can't do that!" Cam shook with the effort of staying down so far. It hadn't seemed hard before, but now that she dwelled on it, she longed more than anything to take in another breath.

"That's the only way, dear. I can lead you if you like."

She couldn't go back. The depths presented the answer.

Seerah dove, her legs kicking strong and sure, and Cam swam after her. Down. Down.

Did she really want this? What would Varin think? Would he think her ugly after this, for sure? Would he want a horizontal lunged girl? A girl who took full breaths? Would he ask her to 'wish him luck' if she towered over him?

Maybe not. But even if he doesn't, I do.

She wanted that for herself. Ever since the truth had come out, that horrible truth that her mother had placed a cage inside her, she'd wanted out of the cage. She swam down, and found the strength to continue, even when her lungs constricted and begged for new air. The pearl grew larger, and larger, and pushed on that metal inside her, and with a burst, broke it inside her. Her body expanded twice as much, her legs lengthened, and her lungs grew to accommodate the pearl inside.

It wasn't hard any more to hold her breath, it was as if she had just jumped in the sea.

"Tell Elaine hello." Seerah smiled. "Maybe . . . maybe I'll visit, now that another woman has broken free."

Cam rushed towards the surface. She couldn't wait to get there and take—

Her! First! Full! Breath!

It tasted like the sweetest honey, when she didn't have to stop herself, but kept inhaling to an impossible vastness. After an interminable amount of time, she brought forth the pearl she'd incubated, and she didn't realize its size until she blinked the pier into view, along with Varin's stare. She soared over him, as tall as he and half, a good nine feet. She handed him the pearl and its circumference spanned wider than his chest.

She waited.

He didn't run.

"I don't care what Elaine thinks anymore," she said. "This is who I am. And I like who I am." She paused. "Now is when you say something."

"You're—you're gorgeous," he said. "I'd always thought you were pretty, but—"

She levered herself onto the pier and bent to throw her arms around him, the pearl between them like an entire backpack full of pearls.

"I wanted to tell you before you dove in," he said. "I'm sorry what your mom did to you. And I'm sorry that—that I said those things. I thought you were watching me to see how I did. I didn't know that you—that you wanted to submerge. I thought I wasn't enough for you."

"I thought I was too much for you," Cam said. "But that doesn't matter to me. Not anymore."

"Let's go and change things," he said in her ear.

They marched up to the council, pearl in hand. Her mother shrieked at Cam, and Cam smirked and just sauntered past her in two giant strides.

"Here," she said, and planted the pearl on the table.

They all gawked at it. Such a large gem would fetch tens of thousands of gold at the market in the valley.

"I have one condition, or I leave and take this with me, and sell it and keep the money." She paused. "First, no girls get inner corsets, ever again." She waited till their gasps died down. "And you allow all those who wish to, to train in breathing exercises, and diving, like the men."

The council looked from her to the pearl and back again. Her uncle laughed into his elbow, then stood beside Cam and clapped her on the back.

"Don't do this!" Her mother said. "Don't you see? You're acting like a man! It's very ugly!"

Now that Cam had grown so tall, her mother's smallness didn't intimidate her so much—didn't make her feel less for being more.

"How strange," Cam said. "I feel more beautiful now than I've ever been." She looked at Varin and smiled. "Size isn't masculine, or feminine. Neither is incubating pearls. I'm who I am, and that's what matters to me."

EMMIE CHRISTIE's work tends to hover around the topics of feminism, mental health, cats, and the speculative, such as unicorns and affordable healthcare. She has been published in Zooscape Magazine *and* Three-Lobed Burning Eye *and she graduated from the Odyssey Writing Workshop in 2013. She also enjoys narrating audiobooks for Audible. You can find her at emmiechristie.com or on Facebook @EmmieChristieFiction or Twitter / Instagram @EmmieChristie33.*

MEMOIR FOUND IN A BULLET

Kyle E Miller

You've probably already been to the place where you will die.

Maybe it's your bathtub or the bed in the quiet room on the second floor of your mom's house—the one that smells like cats and pot-pourri—but it might just as easily be a movie theater, a bar, or a mall. Ordinary places: that's where we die.

In my case, it was a nightclub. I had only been there once before, because I don't like clubs, it's not my scene, but my boyfriend wanted to go. We fought about that and a lot of things that night, and the last thing I ever said to him was, "Well, my mom thought my shoes were cute."

My story is a circle.

It's one of the few types of stories accepted by the general public. It's part of the canon of acceptable narrative shapes. If you tell a story outside the canon, people get upset. I learned about this on my own, on the internet. I'm not an academic, and if I were, I probably wouldn't have to write my story on the inside of a coffin, and it prob-ably wouldn't have to remain here forever, lost in the dark. If I were a scholar, my story might be featured in a journal, reviewed by peers who make approving noises over the pages, nodding to a footnote, harrumphing at a cited source, and making comments like, "I love the imperatives inherent in this piece."

I'm the first one in my family to go to college, but I didn't finish because we ran out of money after my first semester. I don't come from a cultured background. My parents were rednecks, and I'm not ashamed of it. I didn't grow up reading Homer and watching French New Wave films and visiting Rome. I've only read two of Shakespeare's plays, and I don't have an opinion about their authorship. I only speak one language. When I was young I watched old Disney movies on VHS until the tape deteriorated. And because of all this, I hit a wall and blamed it on my own stupidity. A barrier, a limit, a border. I was told I didn't have anything interesting to say. What did some poor white boy know about the world? I worked harder than everyone else around me when I was alive, but the wall is tall and impenetrable. Beyond was success, really *being* someone, having a voice. If only I was smarter, I thought, then I could cross the border and enter that distant country full of people whose voices are heard.

And now I'm stuck inside a wall in a nightclub.

My story is a circle.

We met at a party under the street.

A stream cut through where they wanted the road to be, so they built a bridge over it. Kids liked to gather in the underpass to tag the walls with graffiti and smoke weed. He was already there with his friends, and when I stepped into the gloom of the bridge, I scanned the faces like you do when you're single, and saw him behind a veil of blue smoke. And then his face swam out from behind the smoke and he smiled. Everything was damp from a recent rain, and I could hear a bird bathing in the stream, and in the distance a sound like thunder. I don't remember everything, but I remember this so well.

"We're safe," someone said. "This is the best place to be during a tornado."

There were storms in the forecast, wild ones, with hail and high winds.

"It's not thunder," he said. He would soon be my boyfriend. "It's dynamite. Or trucks dumping stone. There's a quarry nearby," and I thought he said my name. Cory. My face grew warm. My heart jumped. I looked up and smiled, but he was looking at the water, and then I realized what he had actually said, and I blushed even harder and looked away.

Later, we took a walk together downstream, and I almost slipped on the rocks.

"I don't have the right shoes," I said. "For walking on rocks."

"I think they're cute," he said, and he smiled again, his cheeks all wrinkling up. He looked older when he smiled, and I liked that.

The trees bent over the stream on both sides, enclosing it like another underpass. It felt cozy. There was junk in the stream, old garbage bags, the gray fur of a rotted carpet, empty white jugs, the kind used for industrial cleaners and bleach. A few minnows darted away from our feet, and I said I wanted to look for frogs.

We looked, but we didn't find any, and I remembered reading a book for school about the sixth extinction and how frogs were among the first to disappear. I wondered what else might be left out of the future, but I never imagined it would be me.

When we got back to the underpass, a girl came up to us and made kissy noises. She wore an ivory medallion on a leather thong, the ivory embossed with the image of a mermaid flashing its tail, and I remember thinking about a baby elephant chasing birds and saying, "I hope that's not real ivory."

She said, "Don't be a troll," and the guy who would be my boyfriend pointed at the bridge above our heads and said, "Get it?" He laughed and laughed.

Water is the original ecstatic experience. Water is the circle that connects us all. The earth is about 71% water. The human body is 50% to 65% water. We drink each other. We bathe in each other. We dance under the same rain.

Ghosts are a lot like water, it turns out: we adhere, we're sticky, we run in circles, and we disintegrate every surface we touch. We're stuck to the last thing we saw in life with a bond no one can break. Dying taught me a lot, stuff no scholar could ever know. Like no one dies happy. And although no one dies happy, some die in peace, with grace. I didn't, but some do. And they get away, they escape the circle, they don't get stuck. But for all the rest, and it's most people, their bodies give up a ghost and it stays, it adheres, and they spend an eternity trying to come unstuck.

Those who kill themselves haunt their own bodies after death, a true hell: only the self, forever. People who die in a place they have never been haunt that place. Victims of homicide haunt the weapons that kill them, and those who die alone and lonely haunt others, picking away at their lives like vultures. First they circle, and then they strike.

Ghosts are a lot like water. We're everywhere, but most of the time you can't see us.

Isn't it strange how we try to control what others desire? I'm ashamed to say so, but I didn't want my boyfriend to *want* to go to the club. I wanted him to hate it like I did. I was being an idiot. Our differences made me lonely.

I wish I could say I had a premonition that night, or that I saw an omen, a heron flying south or a dead cat on the doorstep, but I was just jealous. I thought he wanted to go to the club to look at other guys. Why else wouldn't we just drink and dance at his apartment?

"It's just not the same," he said, and he pulled on my arm, and I closed down. That's what I do when something makes me uncomfortable: I shut down, draw the curtains, close the doors and windows of my soul. I couldn't help it. You'd have an easier time controlling the weather.

Everything was an argument that night. He spent too much time in the bathroom. We didn't have the right kind of sex. I cried too much.

I wore the wrong shoes. He thought they were ugly and inappropriate for the club. He said they wouldn't even let me in with shoes like that. We argued about my shoes on the last night of my life.

I like to think he's still alive, walking around in my shoes.

Once, my high school chemistry teacher showed us a clip of a high-powered water jet cutting through a piece of sheet metal. I don't know what we were supposed to take away from it, but it never left me. Water is usually associated with healing and rejuvenation, and yet there it was, as destructive and dangerous as a weapon. You could kill someone with it. And then I thought of how I almost died at the foot of a waterfall once, and then I remembered typhoons and waterspouts and tidal waves. Water giveth and water taketh away.

I'll never forget that: a gun shooting water so fast it can cut through lead.

On the shore of a nearby lake, my boyfriend and I took his rowboat out into the cattails. Dragonflies mated on the tips of lily petals, and the oars shed white paint into the water and onto the palms of my hands. Somewhere, a loon called, and I shivered. We heard shouting from the bank. At first I thought it was music. I looked up from the lily pads and saw a little man in black and white waving his arms at the sky and the water, and a group of people behind him.

"Birth control and abortifacients," he shouted. I don't know if he was a preacher, but he sounded like one. There was a rhythm to his words, a sort of harsh musicality. That's how I remember it: a preacher on the bank, his feet in the reeds and muck, ranting about abominations in the water. His audience was a few boatfuls of fishermen, and us. The fish and turtles weren't listening.

"Birth control in the water. Against nature and against God. Abominations." And the last thing we heard him say was, "Must we baptize our babes among transexual fish?" I laughed, and my boyfriend psychologized the man. He liked to try to explain things.

After a while, we stopped rowing, dropped the crusty old anchor, and let the boat drift on its line. We shared some chips and hummus and fed crumbs to the bluegill that snapped at the surface of the water. One of them swallowed a big bite, and a moment later a squiggle shot out of its butt like paint from a tube.

I remember thinking the fish were lucky they all used the same bathroom.

The hydrologic cycle, also known as the water cycle, begins everywhere. It is essential to life on Earth. It's a sort of symphony of water in all of its forms, an ode, a hymn to this essential molecule.

Evaporation from the heat of the sun, condensation as clouds and fog, advection via the winds, precipitation and desublimation, accumulation, all that water running off, some taken by plants to be transpired later, infiltration into the soil, percolation, seepage, erosion of minerals, subduction, evaporation.

Water music.

According to the internet, the cycle is intensifying due to human enterprise, causing greater rainstorms, increased flooding, and more frequent droughts.

The music is getting louder.

There's a phenomenon by which when you hear a new word, you're likely to hear or see it again in the next few days. A few days after the incident at the lake I saw a headline on the internet about male fish laying eggs. I clicked on it, wondering if I had been baptized in a lake full of pregnant male fish. Evidently, girls were flushing birth control pills down toilets, and estrogen was leaking into the water and creating "intersex" fish.

According to the article, antidepressants were also having ill effects on fish. They made them react to predators differently, made them bolder. My antidepressants did the same thing. When I started taking them, I could talk to strangers more easily. But I flushed them down the toilet pretty quickly. They made me dizzy in the morning. My penis lost all sensitivity, I gained weight, and started losing hair. I thought that's what people did with pills, so I flushed them. It seemed somehow final, poetic, even rebellious, but really I was just acting out a scene I had seen in a movie, or a dozen movies. I was fulfilling a cliche. I bet no one flushed their pills down the toilet until they saw it in a movie.

What came first, the fish or the egg?

*

Ghosts are a lot like water. We erode our haunts—people, places, things—with perpetual loops in the dark. We spin and spin, hoping to bore a hole in the wall and escape. Eventually, if I write long and hard enough, I'll write a word deep enough to be a hole, and then I can swim away like the ones who died in peace. That's the second reason I'm doing this. The first is because I want to be heard for once, at last.

Writing is a race against evaporation. There are other forces at work here. I'm forgetting things, even myself. I don't remember what I look like. I don't remember my boyfriend's name. I don't remember my mother's face.

But I remember her paintings.

She painted landscapes. No matter what scene she painted—mountains, meadows, a rural village, or the lake where I was born—it was always raining, sometimes only suggested by the color of the sky, and sometimes as a colorless veil over the whole picture. One time, when she was older and witchier and began to paint less frequently, keeping her bedroom door locked, I snuck in and peeked at her latest painting.

It was raining frogs, a green beaded curtain lowered on the slopes of a mountain.

I don't know if my boyfriend made it out alive. He might be beside me in the dark, or whirling alongside me in the wall opposite. Maybe he's writing a story too, but he would probably call it a work of "creative non-fiction."

One time, he gave me a book to read. He didn't often share them, and after what happened, I think I know why. I think he knew I wouldn't like it. It wasn't even really a story, just a series of vignettes about a writer being drunk and comparing his life and work to that of a bunch of ancient philosophers, myths, and obscure British poets. I told my boyfriend it was the most pretentious thing I had ever read, the most self-indulgent and pompous book on Earth. He ripped it out of my hand and said, "You just don't have the classical education to appreciate it."

He was right.

I wrote when I was alive too. I taught myself and thus was never very good. I wrote a story about a single gay man trying to raise his son in a dystopian world of perpetual rain. The rain wasn't the real antagonist, even though it ate away the roof of their house. Society was the villain. Other people didn't think a boy should grow up with just a gay dad. I wrote it one day when I thought I wanted to be a father, but it was wordy and sentimental, not nearly as good as it sounds. I called it "The Man Who Stopped the Rain" and this is how it started:

"I lived long enough to see the rain eat through the roof and wash away the windows. Little ripples appeared in my soup like tiny fish coming to the surface of their sea of broth and noodles. And then I felt it in my hair and heard the fire crackle and spit and saw my son look up from writing in his journal where the words were running to-gether."

That's kind of like citing a source, isn't it?

I never showed it to my boyfriend. I was too afraid after the first time, when he said, "It's a nice little story, but it's kind of whimsical."

As if that was a bad thing. "There's no room anymore for the nonessential," he said. "Everything needs to mean something now."

Writing filled me with an inescapable urgency. I felt trapped, cornered, and yet never more alive. I wrote so fast my pen went through the paper. I felt possessed. My therapist said it was bipolar disorder, and that I was going through a manic spell. That's the word she used, *spell*. My other therapist, a social worker, said some people learn to love their neuroses. I think I loved mine. It was like having a friendly spirit that came to visit sometimes. He kept me company. He took over for me when I had something to say and wasn't sure how to say it.

When I used to write, I thought I was haunted.

A few weeks after reading the article about the intersex fish, I heard a pundit on the radio in my dad's garage shouting about chemicals in the water. Evidently, the chemicals were turning the frogs gay, and we should be as outraged by that as he was, though he didn't say why. I thought he probably cared more about the fact that the frogs were gay than the chemicals in the water, but then I thought that he probably didn't care about any of it, and that it was all an act, that he really had no convictions at all except the desire to make a fool of his opponents. No one wanted to change the world; they only wanted victory over their enemies. I told my dad to change the station, but he didn't listen. What was my voice against the authority of the media?

That night, I reread the article about the intersex fish. This time, I read all the way to the bottom, and it turned out that scientists knew all about it because they had created their own intersex fish in a lab. The same people who made them in a lab were warning the public not to make them in the wild.

It made me so angry that no one seemed to care, that it was acceptable, because it was science, as if anything done in the name of science was progress. I was in the act of discovering hypocrisy. I asked my boyfriend, "How is this okay?" and he just looked at me and said, "Because science."

Maybe I'm an idiot, but that sounds like just another way of saying God.

I remember thinking it was the music at first, a pulse of bass. I thought the sudden surge of people was just the natural tide of the dance floor. I had a bad feeling about it, a barely perceptible twist in my gut, but I was drunk and when I saw someone on the floor, I laughed and said, "What are you doing down there?"

But then I saw the open door and the glare of streetlights for an instant before it was shrouded by a flood of people streaming out, or trying to anyway, and some were trampled underfoot. I remember thinking that someone should be crying, but no one was, not even myself.

The first thing I did was look for my boyfriend. I was still upset and even thinking about breaking up with him, but I didn't think twice about looking for him. I swear I've never wanted to hold someone so badly. And then I was surprised to find myself being carried through the air and embedded in the wall. I think a few bullets hit me, but the one that killed me went through my body and into the wall. The forensics team or whatever will remove it soon, but I want to be left in peace.

I still don't know who did it, but I don't think I want to know. Some will blame it on someone from far away, even though it happened right here. Others will blame it on our own culture, on the prevalence of guns and hatred. But no one really knows, and it's all just rhetoric, and the blood still struck the floor, and my boyfriend is still alone, and I'm still dead, and the dead don't care to be appropriated for the wars of the living.

One of the things I learned when I died is that life is a study of cycles. Ups and downs. What my therapist would call bipolar. Some summers felt so distant from the summer I lived by a lake and dove for treasure. Almost fifty dollars in paper bills, swimming at the bottom of the lake, bright as fish. Cicadas humming in the gloaming of the most sultry season of my life. I remember feeling light like a dandelion seed. And then the pale, wan summer when I moved back in with my mom, the last summer, when I had no money and could only afford to see my boyfriend once a week, driving so far to see him in the city, the humidity like a damp blanket, and my mom was painting frogs, and we argued about shoes, and we went to the club, and I never saw anyone again.

I remember being afraid of a certain kind of face. It's the face of my uncle, a face common in the town where I grew up. It's usually leering out the rolled down window of a pickup truck: a man, anywhere from thirty to fifty years old, short hair, smugness engraved in the angles of his mouth, sunglasses perched on his head, skin permanently tanned from working outside, almost red in places, and I see him the way most people see a hornet: ready to sting.

I don't know where this comes from. I've rarely been bullied and I was never abused. Well, I was, but not by anyone with a face like that. Maybe I'm imagining it, but there's something about the look this face gives me. It's as if he can peel back the curtain of my bedroom window and he knows—somehow, he *knows*—who I'm sleeping with. And he doesn't approve, and he's so sure of himself and his place in the world that he doesn't mind telling you how much he wishes I didn't exist.

You can't be free if you're still bothered by the mere existence of another person.

After I came out, this fear of faces slowly built until I was afraid to look most men in the eyes, and I was afraid to be myself. My boyfriend made me feel safer, but I began censoring myself.

As if I weren't censored enough already.

transpire (tran-spahyuh r): verb (used without object)

...

4. to be revealed or become known.

"Don't wait for the golden age, the day the rain stops. Never rely on any one particular future for happiness. When the future comes, if it comes at all, there's no telling what will be in it. And what will be left out."

—from "The Man Who Stopped the Rain," page 44

I remember taking a shower in my mom's house after I moved back in. The water smelled like iron, like blood.

I had just lost my job and couldn't find another one, and my boyfriend wasn't allowed to have another person living in his apartment. We argued about that too, but he was always one to follow the rules. "What if they found out?" he would say, as if that would be the end of everything. He had a kind of mania about law and order.

Where I was living before, we had city water, but my mom's house had well water, and it stained everything it touched with rust. Drains and sinks, the whole shower and tub, clothes in the washer, and even the sidewalk outside where water trickles out from a tube when you run a load of laundry. We took precautions, like buying bottled water—everyone did by then—but you couldn't help but shower in the stuff. It made my hair feel brittle, my skin slimy.

I'll never forget buying a brand new bar of soap, leaving it in the shower, and finding it the next morning eaten full of holes, like tunnels bored by worms.

I wondered if the water weren't doing that to our bodies, only more slowly.

I remember the best day of my life. On our first anniversary, my boyfriend gave me a slip of paper with a riddle that, once solved, led to buried treasure. I had to travel to the lake to find it, and he tagged along. The middle of summer. The air was crisp, the sky seemed farther away than usual. It was a diamond day.

I remember being caught in a sudden downpour.

"It's a monkey's wedding!" my boyfriend cried, and we kissed and I thought, we're going to get married.

There are a lot of us now, us ghosts. We're moving faster. We're circling with increasing intensity.

We're all slowly gathering, dripping down, combining, cohering, falling, traveling down, down, always down, down every roof and mountain to a hollow where we can rest. We soak into the earth and disintegrate everything we touch. We evaporate. We sublimate. We transpire. We return as rain.

If I were an academic, a scientist, a celebrity, or a pundit, I wouldn't have to write in the dark. My story would be everywhere. I would have something to say. If I was a sparkling spectacle, if I was simple and stupid and full of profit potential, everyone would love me.

Who can bear the truth? The fact that everything is good and evil, like guns, like water, like ghosts that heal and haunt, protect and slaughter. That everything is more complicated than we care to believe. That our thoughts and stories will always be incomplete. That questions are more necessary than answers. That I loved you deeply even when I didn't. That ghosts cannot write love stories. That I miss you and miss you and miss you.

I'm writing so fast and hard now that one of these periods will finally puncture the wall and create an exit. I'll pour out. There are so many ghosts, more every day, that's the nature of time, of history, but our voices should be as plentiful as water. Our stories should not be rare. They should be honest and true. They should be ours. I don't care if it doesn't mean what you want it to mean, or if it doesn't mean anything at all. I want my voice to return each season like the voices of frogs. I want my stories to be as common as fish in the sea. I want to be synonymous with the falling of rain.

Thrown out of Fairyland for crimes against the Realm, KYLE E. MIL-LER is a naturalist and poet living in Michigan. He can usually be found in the dunes or forests, turning up logs looking for life. Past incarnations include zookeeper, video game critic, retail manager, stable hand, and writing tutor. His fiction has appeared in Clarkesworld, Three-Lobed Burning Eye, *and* Honey & Sulphur.

Acknowledgements

We survived our first year in business! It hasn't always been easy, but it has always been fun. Thank you to everyone who has supported us as a press, whether that be through buying our books, spreading the word, or just generally being lovely. Special thanks this time to Jelena Dunato for her friendship and unwavering support, and for being an amazing co-editor on this project. Thanks also to Dr Sam Hirst for the amazing and very informative introduction!

Much love,

Antonia

MORE FROM GHOST ORCHID PRESS

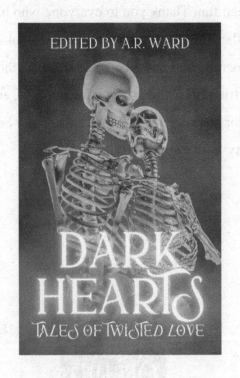

EDITED BY A.R. WARD

DARK HEARTS

TALES OF TWISTED LOVE

ghostorchidpress.com

CPSIA information can be obtained
at www.ICGtesting.com
Printed in the USA
BVHW071623090222
628353BV00004B/161